LEFT UNSAID

LEFT UNSAID

JOAN B. FLOOD

EDITIONS

Cover design by Doowah Design.
Photo of Author by Ayelet Tsabari.

Acknowledgements

This book was printed on Ancient Forest Friendly paper.
Printed and bound in Canada by Hignell Book Printing Inc.

We acknowledge the support of the Canada Council for the Arts and the Manitoba Arts Council for our publishing program.

Library and Archives Canada Cataloguing in Publication

Flood, Joan B., 1949-, author
    Left unsaid / Joan B. Flood.

Issued in print and electronic formats.
ISBN 978-1-77324-009-1 (softcover).
--ISBN 978-1-77324-010-7 (EPUB)

    I. Title.

PS8611.L64L44 2017   C813'.6   C2017-904686-1
                                             C2017-904687-X

Signature Editions
P.O. Box 206, RPO Corydon, Winnipeg, Manitoba, R3M 3S7
www.signature-editions.com

To my mother, Bríd Flood.

Sorry you won't get to read it, but then, you did manage to get white roses on the windowsill that time.

1

MY VISIT WITH MAGGIE HADN'T GONE WELL. SHE'D BEEN agitated and rambling on about the scarf again. Not even the little song she loved calmed her. The Matron dropped in on my visit, which was never a good thing. Either something had gone wrong with Maggie or fees were going up. This time it was the fees. To add to things, the long bus ride home from Dublin was ripe with the smell of wet woollen coats and rattled by coughs and sniffles. Maybe, I thought, I'd catch pneumonia and die and wouldn't have to worry about Maggie, Ma and Da and the farm, and money ever again.

We jounced our way down the country in the wet dark so that by the time we neared Kiltilly I'd almost forgotten a world existed outside the bus's confines. When we reached the village I was weary and loath to go home to the conversation I'd have to have with my mother and father about what to do about money and Maggie. My older sister Maggie had been up in St. Mary's, a private home for the mentally ill in Dublin, for years and we'd mortgaged the farm to the hilt to pay for it. A new increase in fees and we would lose everything. Literally. A hard choice was coming: Maggie or the farm. And what would become of Ma and Da with the farm gone? We'd have to rent a house somewhere for the three of us. There was nothing suitable in the village, and anyway, it would break their hearts to move. It would break what was left of mine, no doubt about it. A rise in fees would come sooner or later,

I'd known. I'd wrestled the questions the last few months when I couldn't sleep, when my past folly was written in plain, luminous letters on the ceiling. *Delia Buckley*, I said to myself then, *you are a madwoman. What were you thinking?* So instead of walking out home right off the bus I stopped by Peggy O'Shea's café and gnawed on the problem as I sat with my tea and apple crumble piled with fresh cream. The cup of tea was steaming hot, just the way I liked it. I tried to put my worries aside for the moment.

The door opened and Daniel Wolfe walked in. I didn't welcome the sight of him. He stood in the doorway, the light catching the raindrops on his ankle-length dark grey coat, his trilby set low on his forehead. Peggy had risen to attention behind the glass cases displaying buns and pastries.

"How are you today, Mr. Wolfe?" she called across. "We don't see you in here too often."

"Fine, fine," he called back.

He walked over to my table like I'd sat there waiting for him. He had changed. Of course he had. It was 1990, not 1968. He took off his hat, shook the rain off it, and held it three fingered at his side. His hair was grey, almost white. He carried a bit of extra weight now and deep lines that held his mouth in parentheses. He still had that air of entitlement he'd always had. Too bad I hadn't been so quick to see that about him when I first met him. But then, I'd only been a girl, really, for all that I was twenty-three years old. Innocent.

"Good day, Delia," he said, as if we'd spoken to each other on a regular basis, which we hadn't. Even though we lived in the same small village we had gone years without meeting directly or speaking. He was often away on book tours or travelling. When he was in the village he didn't exactly hang around. He had someone to shop and fetch for him. Besides, we didn't travel in the same social circles, him being part of the gentry and me being a villager. "May I sit with you?"

He touched the back of the chair across the table. I was about to say no, but Peggy had her eyes out on sticks on us from behind the counter, so I nodded. He settled himself into the seat and Peggy was beside him in a flash taking his order for coffee and a scone. I stayed silent when she left, giving him nothing. He sat back in his chair, comfortable as if in his own living room. We stayed that way until Peggy delivered his cup of coffee to the table. She wiped away imaginary crumbs with a cloth that left wet streaks behind, but as neither of us said a word she had no option but to move off and take up her task of overseeing things from behind the counter.

"Delia," he said again when we were alone. He stirred sugar into his coffee. After a long draw on his cup and a shift in his chair, he spoke again.

"Look, Delia, I'm sorry for the past, how it was. Believe me, I am."

Not nearly as sorry as I am, I thought. I sipped my tea. It had cooled off and gone bitter.

"I've come to see you because I want to make amends. And to ask something of you."

"You think you can make amends?"

It came out like the hiss of a scalded cat. I clamped my lips tightly around my teeth and sat back in the chair.

"No. Not really, but I can help you now. I know how things are with the farm." The whole country probably knew how deeply in debt the farm was. I said nothing, though it embarrassed me that Daniel Wolfe would know about my family affairs. He sat for a moment, then continued. "And you can help me. I'm willing to pay you well, Delia, more than well. Please hear me out."

He hadn't changed, then. He still believed he could buy his way in and out of anything. I listened to his proposition all the same, too full of curiosity not to. I wondered how he knew where to find me. Mind you, it was my habit to go up to visit Maggie almost every week. Everyone in the village knew that. Nobody drove to Dublin because of the congestion on the carriageway and hassle of parking when they got there, but today I wished I had taken my car. Everyone knew, too, when the evening bus arrived. Still, it was unnerving to think he must have been waiting for me.

"I've got cancer, Delia. Riddled with it. There's nothing to be done for me."

"What cancer? How bad is it?"

The nurse in me couldn't help but ask.

"Esophageal. Stage IV. I've six, maybe twelve months at best. Right now I'm deciding on what treatment, if any. I don't want to spend the time I have sick from treatment that ultimately won't work."

Not many people opted for none. His decision surprised me, as I thought of him as a person who put himself first at all times. Maybe that's what he was doing, opting for a possibly shorter but better-quality life.

"Maybe treatment will cure you," I said.

"You're a nurse, Delia. You know how unlikely that is."

He was right. Still, you had to offer hope. He wanted me to care for him because he knew me, trusted me, he said. Please, he said. I wanted to tell him no, to walk away, turn my back on him the way he'd done to me those years ago. He offered a lot of money. I told him I'd think about it.

"That's all I ask, Delia. That's good enough," he said.

I WALKED OUT OF THE VILLAGE ON THE LIMERICK ROAD. IT WAS a walk I loved in any weather. I had grown up in Kiltilly and lived in the same farmhouse just outside the village all my life except for the few months I spent in Wales years ago, when I was in my early twenties. I knew to within a week when the lilac in Mrs. Green's garden would bloom each spring and how bountiful the conkers would be in autumn by the blossoms on the horse chestnut in May. I'd watched the martins gather on the electric wires for their migration every year since I was a little girl, their chattering drowning out the other birds, and the eerie silence when they'd left on their long migration and the cold descended on the land. I had celebrated my greatest joy, grieved my worst nightmare, and vented my most awful sufferings on this road. I'd come this way after a patient's death, weary in my bones, and felt my spirit lighten at the sight of our modest farmhouse nestled below the rise of the meadow.

This night my heart did not lighten when, through the bare winter trees, I first saw the light from our farmhouse. I stopped at the side of the road as the rain pelted down with renewed force and filled my nose with the earthy smell of turf carried from chimney smoke. It was there in the dark, the light from my home showing me the way forward, that I came up with my scheme to keep Maggie where she was and save the farm. If Daniel agreed and it turned out to cost me sleep for a while, well, there was plenty to keep me awake anyway.

2

"HELLO, I'M BACK," I CALLED AS I OPENED THE FRONT DOOR. MY mouth watered at the smell of onions and potatoes, mutton and thyme that greeted me.

"Well, how was she? Was the bus late? We're just having our tea and I kept a bit of dinner for you. Before you get your coat off go find your father, see if he's nearly done with the milking. It's too much for him, really, it is."

Mam rattled it all off without waiting for an answer. I didn't even try, simply went right out the back door to find Da. He was in the shed milking the last of our few cows by hand. The sweetish smell of warm milk permeated the air. He squatted on a stool, head against a cow's flank, hands pumping rhythmically.

"Tea's ready," I said.

"Aye, I'll be right in, five minutes. I'll not keep you. Keep your news for me, right?" He didn't turn. His hands kept their rhythm as the milk hissed into the bucket. He loved those cows, and I thought him happier since we were down to only a few that he could milk the old-fashioned way. He wouldn't last long if we moved away with nothing to occupy his hands. I patted his shoulder and went back to the house.

☙

"SHE'S MUCH THE SAME," I REPORTED OVER THE MEAL. "SHE seems well enough, wandering a bit, as usual. Probably tired, the nurse said. She's not better, that's for sure."

We had never expected Maggie to need care for so long. When she first became ill we were sure she'd get over it. We even had her home with us a few times, but each time she deteriorated to the point Mam couldn't cope on her own. We never did have an explanation for her condition that made sense to me as a nurse, but as her sister who knew her well I understood her state.

"I need to get up to see her," Da said. He'd been saying that for years. He'd never go. Maggie didn't recognize him, and he couldn't take it. He always sent her sweets, though, and still managed to find the ones coated with soft sugar she'd loved as a child.

"The fees are going up again."

Mam concentrated on spreading a thick slab of butter onto her bread. Da put his cup down and looked at me.

"What? They just went up not so long ago. How much?" he asked.

"Enough," I said. Telling the exact amount would make no difference anyway as the level was just about over our heads as it was.

Mam wiped her mouth with the back of her hand. "I don't know. We can't keep it up. I don't know what we're to do."

"I can go to the bank tomorrow. Maybe we..." Da left the rest unsaid.

"We can't," Mam said. "We've used up all we can. The manager warned about that last time."

"Jesus."

"Don't swear." It was my mother's automatic response to swearing of any kind.

"Well, if there was a time to, it's now. "

"Maybe we should look for somewhere else for her, outside Dublin, like. It would cost less." Her voice was flat with defeat. It was a familiar round for us.

"But, sure we searched high and low last year. Everywhere was full and they were awful places anyway. Not enough staff. They know her in St. Mary's. She knows them," I reminded them. Reminded myself.

Mam put her fork and knife down and lined them up neatly on her plate.

"Your father and I talked about all this after last time. I don't know what else we can do. We can't go on. Could we have her at home, do you think?"

"Jesus, no. We tried that before. She needs looking after all the time. Who'll do it? You and Da can't and I'm not even at home some evenings when I work. I'm not even in Kiltilly sometimes. Getting someone in would cost more than where she is."

"We could sell the farm," Da said.

Mam and I stared at him in silence.

"We could," he said again. His eyes were on his plate as he spread raspberry jam on his bread.

"No. We can't."

Da looked up at my sharp tone. We stared each other down a moment, then Da cut his slice of bread in two.

"Who'll take it on when your mother and I are gone anyway?"

"I will. You know I love it here." I was surprised I even had to say it.

"You have your own work, you couldn't run the farm," Mam said. "Could you?"

"Maybe not, but I can keep the land in the family. Besides, most of what we'd get if we sold would go to the bank."

"Well, you'll have to make a hard decision right off the top," Da said. "It's the farm or Maggie now, isn't it?"

"Let me think about it for a couple of days. I might be able to come up with something."

"If ye can ye're a miracle worker," Da said. "Haven't ye done everything all along?"

"Well, just wait a few days, ok? "

He patted his shirt pocket for his glasses and gathered up the paper.

⚭

"DANIEL WOLFE IS ILL AND WANTS ME TO LOOK AFTER HIM. AS A private nurse, like. He offered good money," I told my mother when Da was out of earshot. The words were out of my mouth before I meant them to be. We were at the kitchen table with a last cup of tea before getting on with the dishes. Mam's head swivelled toward me. I tried not to squirm like a schoolgirl under her gaze, and not for the first time I wondered how much she knew about Daniel Wolfe and me.

"Daniel Wolfe? What does he want with looking after?"

"He's sick. He wants me to come up to the house and look after him. The trouble is, he won't last long, so we'll be back talking about this again before a year passes. But it's another year. Maybe we can figure something out in that time."

Mam got up and emptied the teapot into the sink.

"You can't be seriously thinking of it, surely? That man! After the trouble he caused Maggie," she said. "When were you discussing this with him? Sure, he's hardly ever in the village."

"Trouble he caused Maggie? What do you mean?"

"I don't know exactly what went on, but he has something to do with Maggie's state. I'm not a fool, you know. She makes no sense most of the time, but I can pick up the gist."

"I told you, Mam, Maggie had nothing to do with him as far as I know. She'd have told me if she did," I said.

"Well, he's mixed up in it somewhere. I'm certain of that. When did he talk to you?"

She sat back down at the table and fiddled with her teacup. Her wedding ring was loose on her finger and rattled against the china. She's getting old, I thought. I reached across the table and touched her hand.

"I stopped off at the café when I came down. He was there, and he asked me. It would help us out, Mam. "

"Well, I hope you said no."

"I said I'd think about it. The money is good. Maybe I'll say yes. It means I won't be here too much for the next few months. Can ye get on without me?"

"Of course we can, pet. It's your work. Haven't we always got on without you when you're at your work?"

I WALKED UP THE BACK FIELD JUST AFTER DAWN. I MISSED THE old dog, wished she were still alive. The company would be welcome. Sleep had been erratic, interrupted by my nightmare of being caught in coloured gauze, careening around trying to save myself from something. I'd woken fighting with the air, my hair drenched in sweat. Next I dreamed of Maggie, her arms outstretched calling for baby, baby, but there was none to give her.

The climb to the top of the hill felt like a trek in lead boots. At the top I turned a complete circle, then stopped, facing our farmhouse below. Set back a bit from the road, it seemed part of the earth; the yellow wash on the walls gave it a spring-like air even in the grey winter light. A couple of hens scrabbled in the yard. I was born and grew up in that house. Daniel's offer turned over in my mind. I was well respected and liked as a private care nurse so no one would think it odd I went to work for him. Agency work was always available but offered nothing like the money Daniel Wolfe did. It would gall me to have anything to do with him, but double my usual rates for three or four months would let us keep Maggie in the home for another six or nine months at least. What would happen when that job was gone? We were in dire need of something more than a good wage for a few months. If Daniel Wolfe wanted me to look after him, my price was his help to secure a reasonable mortgage on the farm, no matter what the banks told us. He was a very rich man and well connected. And he owed me something more, more than *I'm sorry*, whether he recognized that or not. Much as it rankled to ask him for anything, I would do it. For Maggie's sake. For the sake of the farm, too, but mostly for Maggie.

NEXT DAY AT PRECISELY HALF PAST TWO I WAS ON DANIEL'S doorstep. It was called the Big House in the village for a reason. It was huge, compared with village abodes, and stood on acres of land. The house had been in the FitzGibbons family for generations and came to Daniel only after his wife, Ellen, died. Between what he inherited from her and the sale of his books, he was a very rich man. The entire cost of our farm would hardly make a dent in his interest earnings, I reckoned. I'd never been inside his house, and never wanted to be. When I was a child, the Wolfes had thrown a summer party for the village children each year, but it was strictly an outdoor affair held on the grounds. It had been madly exciting. There were magicians and a merry-go-round. There were all kinds of treats and sweet sugary drinks, lemonade and orange, the kinds of things that we had at home only on Christmas or birthdays. Each child was sent home with a two-layer-deep box of rich chocolates. Standing on the doorstep, I felt like a child again before the heavy wooden door painted an ugly brown. I felt small. *I'm not a beggar*, I reminded myself. Even then, I could have changed my mind and left, and I almost did. My sense of responsibility for Maggie took over, so I took a deep breath and pressed the bell. From where I stood I caught the faint echo of a Westminster chime from somewhere inside.

Daniel himself opened the door. He was all smiles.

"Come in, come in."

He moved me down the hallway and into the parlour. Though earlier I'd been curious about his house, I was too nervous to take in the room, except to notice the warmth from the fire lit in the grate. He gestured me toward one of the enormous soft armchairs next to the hearth.

"Warm yourself, it's a wickedly cold day. I'll make some tea."

"No, thank you. Wait. I've got a proposition for you."

No use beating about the bush. Besides, if he said no, I didn't want to be sitting with a cup of tea in my hand. I put it to him straight. If he wanted to "make things up" to me and have me look after him until the end, he had to help us get a reasonable mortgage on the farm.

"It's Maggie's care," I told him. "She's settled in St. Mary's. She's used to it. The only other options are one of those small private understaffed places in the middle of nowhere or a locked ward in some hospital. Every penny we have between us goes to the home. The farm belongs mostly to the bank these days. They won't remortgage."

"Your father still works the place?"

"A few cows and chickens left, that's all. He's in his seventies, too old to run the full farm now. We let out a couple of fields to Sam Ryan for grazing. It helps keep things afloat for now."

"And with a reasonable mortgage? You could manage the fees then?"

"With what I earn we'd be fine for a good while. It's the mortgage is killing us."

Silence settled between us. Sunlight shafted into the room and the dust motes floated lazily down the beam.

"I'll do as you ask, Delia. I'll take the mortgage on the farm myself. We'll settle on small enough payment. Even when I'm gone I'll see you right, make sure you can always afford it."

The tension I'd been holding almost released into tears, but I managed to appear calm. I'd at least expected him to think about, maybe even haggle, if not outright refuse.

"Why do you want me to take care of you?" I was genuinely curious.

"I know you. Well, knew you. Delia, I don't imagine your entire character has changed. Let's say I trust you. Besides, I've checked, and by all accounts you're the best nurse for the job in the whole place. I don't want a total stranger here day in and day out. Please?"

To tell the truth it would have given me great satisfaction to say no, to deny him something he wanted, but I reminded myself it was for Maggie. There was justice in his paying to support her. My silence provoked him to plead, which gave me some mean satisfaction.

"Can't we put the past behind us in this, Delia? It was all so very long ago. I was out of my mind after Ellen died. Then Fran went missing. I didn't behave well, I know that. I was a louse."

I nearly turned and left right then. What did he know of my life? We hadn't kept in touch at all, and I didn't flatter myself that he kept up with what was going on for me. Even if he did, he'd not know everything.

"Is that it, because you were a louse?"

"I know I treated you shabbily. It's been on my mind. A lot of things have been on my mind these last few weeks since I got my death sentence. A long time has passed, I know, but I do want to make some kind of amends and die in peace. And I do trust you to take care of me well. Your reputation stands high in these parts. Very high."

"A lot you care about my reputation."

As soon as the words were out of my mouth I was sorry. Clearly, if I worked for him I'd have to keep control of my tongue.

"Look, Delia, I'll meet your terms. And pay you what I offered at first too, if you'll come up every day for a while, at least until Jude comes. If she does. I'll draw everything up properly with my solicitor about the farm."

I wasn't expecting this. Being his housekeeper wasn't what all my training had been for. Besides, I'd no great skill at it. I told him so.

"Of course not," he said. "Mrs. Conway comes in a couple of days a week and takes care of the house. I know you have great nursing skills, but I'm all alone here and find my own company, well, not the best at the moment. Will you do it for me? Please?"

"Where's your daughter now?"

"She's away in Canada. Vancouver. Married a fellow out there. I'll have to tell her what's going on with me sooner or later. I hope she'll come. We haven't seen eye to eye these past years. She needs to come back and learn how to manage the estate. It'll be all hers after I'm gone. Jude is the only family left. It was her sister who had the interest in it, but…"

He didn't finish the sentence. His older daughter, Fran, disappeared not long after his wife died. A horn blast from a ship leaving the harbour cut the silence between us and a yearning to be anywhere else on earth yawned inside me. I wanted to have nothing more to do with this family. Nothing. But there was never any real chance I'd say no. I knew that from the moment he agreed to my terms. There was too much on the line for me, but I wasn't about to let him know that. All the same I felt angry and trapped. I'd be months tied to this man. Maybe even a year, but that was unlikely. He'd told me his test results before we'd left the café.

I nodded my agreement.

"Let's have a drink then, to seal the deal."

While Daniel was rummaging in the drinks cabinet, I took a look around. The room wasn't what I'd expected, not in any way modern. It was, in fact, stuck somewhere in the late sixties or early seventies. A beige shag carpet covered the floor, faded except for where the edges met the walls. The settee and chairs were a velour-type fabric in dark brown, the seat too deep to be comfortable without several cushions behind your back. Flocked wallpaper in orange, yellow and beige tweed-type pattern covered the walls, except for the chimneybreast, which wore a gold leaf pattern. It was probably the thing in its day, but that day was long gone. A line of photos stood to attention on the mantelpiece. One of Jude at her wedding, with her husband, a tall, weedy fellow with a too-thin face and black eyebrows that arched over brown eyes like he was amazed to find himself there. The couple was flanked by a man and a woman, his mother and father most likely, on one side, and Daniel on the other. There was no corresponding female to represent Jude's mother. Everyone in the photo looked stiff and edgy, except Jude, who seemed perfectly relaxed and happy. There were photos of Daniel, his two daughters Fran and Jude, and his wife Ellen from when the children were younger, about ten and twelve. There was only one photo of Fran as a young woman, her red hair caught by the sun as she stood under a tree. Daniel handed me a glass with an inch of whiskey at the bottom.

"I'm not much of a drinker," I said.

"Just to seal the deal."

Before Daniel could clink my glass with his I raised mine in a salute then took a sip. The liquid lit up my mouth and burned down into my chest.

&

IT TOOK ME MORE THAN A WEEK TO BRING THE MATTER UP with Da and Mam. It was a Sunday afternoon and we were settled into the front room. The papers were ready, Daniel had seen to that, but if my father didn't agree, I was sunk. I told them they had a big decision to make and we should talk. The two of them exchanged glances. Da took his glasses off, folded up the newspaper and put it on the floor next to his feet.

"Well, what is it?" Mam fidgeted her dress down over her knees.

"I've solved the problem of money."

They both straightened themselves on the couch, spines not touching the backrest.

"How so?"

"Daniel Wolfe has agreed to assume the mortgage for the farm. He'll charge no interest, and intends to set a very reasonable monthly amount."

The two of them looked at each other, then back at me as if I'd grown two heads.

"Why would he do that?" my father asked. "What interest does he have in the farm? Hasn't he land enough up there?"

"He wants me to look after him. We were talking about an arrangement and I told him about the farm being in hock and Maggie needing the stability of where she is. He offered."

It wasn't exactly a lie.

"But why? I know you're a skilled nurse, girl, but that's one big payment. It doesn't make sense."

It didn't, that was the trouble. My father was no fool, and he couldn't see someone like Daniel Wolfe giving his money away. Mam cut in before I could answer.

"Because she's young enough to earn it out. What'll happen to us?"

"Oh, Mam, everything will stay the same. The deed will still be in your names. It's just that the mortgage will be held by Daniel Wolfe instead of the bank. I've got papers for you to look at. You're guaranteed a place here until the end of your days. Nothing will change except we won't need to worry about Maggie's care. We can stop worrying about it all."

"And what happens when he goes? Will his heirs want the money back? Or want to get their hands on the farm?" my father asked.

"It will stay with us. Look, you can look over the papers. Take them in to a solicitor in Limerick before you sign them. Even when he dies he's set it up so no increase can happen and the mortgage can't be foreclosed."

I still didn't trust that man at all, but I had given the agreement a good read myself. It certainly looked watertight. I would be relieved when the solicitor looked it over.

"Have a look anyway, Joe. It'll be great not to have to worry about Maggie and the farm, won't it?" My mother held out her hand for the papers. Da stepped forward and took them from me.

"I'll have a look. Your mother and I will talk on it tonight."

The papers trembled in his hand as he turned and left the room.

"I hope you know what you're doing," Mam said.

"Sure, there's no downside to it. Except that I'll be working for Mr. Wolfe for the next while."

"I'm no fool, Delia. I know something is going on. Just watch yourself. The likes of the Wolfes make sure their own nest is feathered every time. I just hope you haven't sold your very soul to them."

In the end, of course, they agreed. Within a week the papers were approved by their solicitor and signed by the two of them.

Knowing we could live our whole lives on the farm without worry put a real lightness in my step that even Mam's tight-lipped disapproval couldn't squash. What choice did any of us have in the long run? It was up to me then to fulfill the bargain and look after Daniel Wolfe.

3

ON FEBRUARY 1, ST. BRIDGET'S DAY, DRESSED IN MY MOST formal outfit and well wrapped up against the raw day, I walked in through the village to take up my new post. Mam thought I should drive so I didn't show up "looking like a pauper," but it wasn't much farther than the village and, as always, I preferred to walk. Days were lengthening and the land was visibly waking despite the lingering cold. It was a blustery morning, the daffodils that had bloomed under the trees tossed on the wind and the bare branches rattled overhead like old bones. It was early still, so the village was quiet, not many people about apart from the small crowd waiting for the bus to take them to work in the city. I fingered Daniel's key in my pocket and my mind took up an old rhyme from childhood, "Ring-a-ring of Roses."

As I went through the gate to the estate my scarf, undone by the wind, blew up over my face and I gave an involuntary yelp of fright as I swiped it away. It caught on the rough iron of the gate and yanked me to a stop, I loosened it and waited for my fright to settle, trying to persuade myself it was not a bad omen, and continued up the long driveway to the house.

The land being a bit higher here than the farm, the gardens were still in late winter mode, just a few snowdrops and crocus scattered at the edge of the path. The heavens opened as I reached the door, so I wasted no time having second thoughts on the step. The key turned easily in the lock.

It was gloomy inside, the curtains still drawn against the night. I went first to the parlour, the only room I knew. I opened

the curtains and paused to admire the oak and poplar trees that
sheltered the lawn the rain was attempting to turn into a pool.
I listened to the house, the strike of rain on the window, the
small creaks as the wind whipped around it. It had a stale, musky
smell, and a neglected kind of quietness that felt heavy, even sad.
A house like this needed some light and love. It was made for
family, but as far as I knew it had been mostly empty for the
past twenty years or so, except whenever Daniel was at home,
which wasn't often or for long. No wonder he didn't want to be
here alone. A renewal of the downpour sent me away from the
window to find the kitchen.

It was a large room with a beautiful oak table and chairs
taking up the area near the window. An electric kettle sat next to
the stove. I filled it and plugged it in before I took my coat off.
I had no idea what Daniel Wolfe liked for breakfast these days.
I remembered days of hotel hot breakfasts eaten well into the
afternoon, and wondered if he rose late or early. An examination
of the fridge revealed nothing much inside: a few eggs, a carton
of milk, a bottle of gin lying on its side, and a tomato that should
have been thrown out about two days before. The bread bin had
a heel of bread that might be all right toasted. In the absence
of knowing what to do next, I made myself a cup of tea, sniffed
the milk and, deciding it was all right, poured a dollop into my
tea. I sat at the table and listened to the wind batter the house
looking for purchase and waited for Daniel Wolfe to put in an
appearance.

4

FOR THE NEXT MONTH, EXCEPT FOR SUNDAYS, I SPENT FROM noon to around eight o'clock at the Big House sheltered behind the yew hedge at the eastern end of the village. In the mornings Daniel worked alone in his study. Complications set in right away. Idleness, I found, didn't suit me. Those first mornings at home I haunted Mam as she went about collecting eggs from the hens, feeding them, and making sure they had water, cleaning out their boxes and checking the run was secure against foxes.

"Why don't you do something nice for yourself?" she asked more than once, tired of me traipsing around after her. "Or take up knitting, or something." It wasn't much different with Da. He was happy enough to have me around, but was content to tend the garden and milk the cows by himself. It did cross my mind to find some morning hours, maybe in the hospital in Limerick.

"Ah, take a bit of a rest," Mam said when I mentioned it to her. "You haven't really had much time off these last years."

It was true. I'd worked every hour possible to pay for Maggie's care and to keep Mam, Da and myself afloat. Sure, we earned some money from the meadows Da let out, and they had a small government pension, but it wasn't nearly enough to cover our expenses.

At a loss, I took to walking out in the morning, sometimes across the fields near the farm, sometimes into the village. Once I wandered up the hill on the road to Killdeara. It was where Maggie and I used to lie on our backs and watch the clouds drift above us on summer afternoons when were growing up. It was where she told me she had decided to become a nun, and asked me if

I thought it was the right thing for her. I didn't, mostly because I couldn't imagine anyone wanting to be shut away in a convent and governed by the rules of a Reverend Mother. Maggie laughed when I told her that. "It's not for everyone," she said. Mam and Da would be ecstatic. There was nothing quite like having a son a priest or a daughter a nun to cheer up Irish parents, but the idea of not having Maggie around saddened me. She was older than me by a good few years, but we were fast friends as well as sisters. I idolized her. It was on this hill too that we talked when she left the convent. The rigours had proven too much for her. "A nervous disposition, not suitable," the Reverend Mother said. She was packed home after three years, thin and pale, with nothing but the clothes she stood up in.

"What went wrong?" I asked her. "What happened?"

She shrugged, her eyes on the village that lay out below us. "Nothing special. I felt confined, just like you said. All that praying drove me mad, or very nearly. I want life around me, children someday."

It didn't quite work out like that for her. She had lived for over twenty years now in a nursing home for the mentally ill.

This morning a small freighter sailed into the harbour led by a pilot, and delivery vans trundled to a stop outside the main shops. A sudden shiver passed through me as I watched the village below me get into the swing of the day. What would people think of me if they knew the truth about me? About Maggie? I pulled my coat around me and started back down the hill.

TWICE A WEEK MRS. CONWAY ARRIVED BEARING GROCERIES AND did whatever tidying up needed doing in the Big House. Our paths rarely crossed, or if we did meet it was only for ten minutes or so at a time. Some afternoons Daniel was shut away for a couple of hours again in his office at work on his book while I did some mending I brought from home. Boredom was weighing on me, and my mind roved too often over what might have been.

One afternoon I took a tour of the house, thinking that had Daniel stood by me after his wife died, I would have been mistress here. It was, by comparison to the farm, huge; two stories high and a basement that housed old furniture and boilers. The kitchen was large enough to seat a family of six or eight, and the dining room was twice that size. Besides these rooms the ground floor had a small toilet, a large draughty hallway, the parlour and two other rooms, one of which was Daniel's office. Upstairs there was a bathroom with a six-foot long bathtub, and six bedrooms. The whole place was spotlessly clean, thanks to Mrs. Conway, but nonetheless had an unlived in air, except for Daniel's bedroom. I didn't go in past the door of that room. From what I could see it was tidy enough but clearly was a male domain, dominated by a double bed with sturdy brown posts. Examining it, I was suddenly lonely for the warmth and shabby comfort of our farm.

ANY AFTERNOON THE WEATHER WAS DECENT I TOOK A CUP OF tea out back to a spot sheltered by the eaves. It overlooked the garden and offered some cover from the drizzling rain that fell at that time of year. Most afternoons Daniel joined me there.

"Can't we be friends, Delia?" Daniel said to me one afternoon. We had been tiptoeing around each other for three weeks with exaggerated formality.

"I'm your employee, not your friend."

"We were more than friends once. We can't pretend the past didn't happen. I should have stuck by you. I know that now. I did care about you, but when Ellen died, the girls needed me. That's what I thought."

I studied him there in the afternoon light and saw how his skin had become looser and duller even in the few weeks since I'd been here. I had forgotten his charm, his easy warm manner, the way he focused on you as if you were the most important person in the world. In spite of myself I was drawn to him, and so as not to show it I was more reserved with him than I usually was with people I nursed.

"I'm sorry, Delia," he said.

There was no pretending it all didn't happen for me. I'd lived with it day in, day out for over twenty years while he was oblivious to the consequences. I could have told him everything then, or part of it.

The breeze brought the scent of lilac on the wind now and again. The sweetness in the air reminded me of those days long ago when Daniel and I were in love.

We were in love, no matter what happened later. I was over the moon, lost in the utter wonder of first love. I knew he was married. Of course I did. And it was never that I pursued him, rather he did me. I was flattered and enjoyed his company. By the time of our first kiss I already loved him. Maggie had a flat in Dublin then, in Ranelagh, and my visits to her doubled as time to spend with Daniel.

"He's married, you know," Maggie said when I first told her I wasn't staying overnight with her.

"Only a Protestant one," I answered.

Maggie gave me a look from under her brows.

"No matter what the Catholic Church has to say about it, it's still a marriage."

Carried away with my feelings, I didn't think of it that way. I chose instead to tell myself it was no true marriage so it was no sin to be seeing him. The no-sex-outside-marriage bit I ignored. Wasn't life opening up in 1967, the old ways going? It was all free love and women's lib.

It seemed a long time ago now.

"Sorry about what?" I asked Daniel.

"That I didn't marry you when Ellen died. I should have done that."

The wind whipped up a bit. I drew my cardigan from the back of the chair and put it on. I said nothing. What could I say that I hadn't already said? I didn't want to talk about Ellen's death, the day that brought an end to my dreams of life with Daniel.

⟨⟩

ELLEN WOLFE DIED ONE COLD DECEMBER NIGHT IN 1967. ABOUT eleven o'clock at night a friend of Da's, seeing the light still on in the house, dropped in to tell us that there had been a terrible accident about ten miles down the road. Mrs. Wolfe's car had been on the wrong side of the road and swerved to avoid hitting Bob Kenney's van head on. She went straight into a telegraph pole. Bob went to help her, but she was, he said, killed dead instantly.

I wanted to call Daniel right away. The nearest phone was at a neighbour's on the edge of the village, but I couldn't call from there. It would have to be the phone box in the high street. It was near midnight by then so I put off phoning until the next day.

As soon as I could I slipped out of work to the call box down by the bus stop. I'd never called him at home before. Most of our contact was prearranged on our dates or he'd call Maggie if there was a change of plan and she'd let me know. My hands shook as I dialled. The phone rang eight or nine times.

One of his daughters answered, the older one, Fran, I thought. I listened to her footsteps go in search of Daniel, through the silence that followed, and more footsteps, growing louder this time, before Daniel's voice came on the line.

"I'm so sorry, Daniel. So very sorry," I said.

"Thank you."

The stark formality of his tone shocked me. He could have been speaking to a complete stranger.

"Daniel?"

"There is nothing to say, Delia. This has been a terrible shock."

He didn't sound like himself at all. I wanted to be there, hold him, comfort him.

"It has, indeed. Can we meet, even for a moment? I would love to see you, make sure you are all right."

Silence stretched out across the line. For a moment I heard voices in the background, then silence again.

"Please, Daniel?"

"Yes, later. I'll pick you up at the usual spot. About ten, okay? We'll talk then."

The day was agony to get through. I swear all the clocks at the hospital were slow. Twice I went to fetch something from the supply room and forgot what I was looking for. I got off my shift at eight o'clock and went home. All the talk in the house was about the accident. Speculation about what had happened, and what would happen to the house and the family fortune, pity for Daniel and her daughters. It was almost unbearable.

He was late, in the end. I waited, wrapped in my warmest coat in the dark under the big pine at the turn of the road, the place he had stopped for me the first night we drove in to Limerick. It had become the spot we'd meet now and then when time between meetings became unbearably long. By the time he arrived I was chilled to the bone. He didn't lean over to open the door for me, so I opened it myself and got into the passenger seat. Before I could say a word, he spoke.

"Delia, we'd better not see each other for a while."

I turned in my seat to look at him. He stared straight out through the windshield.

"What do you mean, a while? Until after the funeral?"

I touched his arm, desperate to get him to look at me so I could read his face. He kept his eyes fixed dead ahead on the night outside. Silence stretched between us, rubbing my nerves raw.

"You must see, Delia, it's not right for us now. The girls just lost their mother. They need time. We all do. I can't be marrying as soon as she's in her grave. I need to do the right thing here."

"The right thing? Are you suggesting we break it off? What about your child I'm carrying? That one needs you to do the right thing too."

Thoughts tumbled around my head. We had planned to spend the next weekend in Galway, three whole days together, to celebrate the baby and plan our life. I knew we needed to change plans now, we did, but his attitude suggested a bigger change. He sat back in the seat and slapped his hands against his knees, the sound sharp enough to make me jump.

"Jesus! Don't you know we can't have a baby now?"

Afraid and angry, I began to babble.

"We can't stop it now, it's too late. It's already here inside me. I know this is a terrible event that's happened and the timing is terrible but we can't not deal with this."

"Hush, Delia."

He finally turned towards me, really looked at me for the first time. He caught my hand as he tried to calm me down.

"Shhh. Don't worry. I'll arrange things. I know a man in London."

"What does a man in London have to do with it?"

"He'll fix you up. You must see, Delia, we can't get married now. Not for a year or so at least. I'll take care of it all. You have nothing to worry about."

Comprehension dawned on me. It would never have occurred to me that Daniel would want to kill his own child, or that, after all the talks we'd had about the rules of the Catholic Church, he'd think I would agree to an abortion.

"Daniel, I can't. I'm a Catholic. Besides, I want your child, our child."

"And I do too. Later. After Fran and Jude settle down. You must see I can't land a wife on them now. It wouldn't be fair. Nor on you either."

I never thought of myself as something that could be landed on anyone. A chill settled in my bones.

"You can't mean that, Daniel. What will happen to me? To our child? You can't just turn away from us now."

He reached inside his overcoat and took out a pen. Then after another root around in his jacket pocket he produced a chequebook. I snatched it out of his hand and tossed it into the back seat.

"You can't buy me off."

Daniel flinched, but wouldn't meet my eye. I was too shocked to cry, but could feel the choke of tears.

"Look at me, Daniel. Look at me."

The words echoed around inside the car. Daniel didn't look at me. Instead he said the words that ended everything.

"Delia, be reasonable."

I waited a minute. When he said nothing else, I yanked open the car door, got out. I have no memory of getting back home.

A week later I got a big cheque in the mail from him along with the name and address of a doctor in London. There was nothing else in the envelope. We never spoke again until a month ago when he found me in the café.

SO DANIEL'S APOLOGY DIDN'T WARM MY HEART MUCH ALL THESE years later.

"Too late for regrets now," I say.

"Delia, I know. I know. But I want you to know I'm sorry. Sorry too that I pressured you to get rid of the child."

"No point in harking to the past," I told him. "It's gone."

He reached out as if he would touch me, but I stood up and gathered up the cups. He crammed his hands into his pockets.

"It is indeed. That's the thing, Delia. Time is very short. Let's not waste it with grudges."

I couldn't forgive him. Yet some small thing thawed in me all the same. He wasn't too long for the world. We'd got that news with his latest tests. The cancer was galloping through him faster than anyone thought it would.

"We can be civil, anyway," I said.

I GOT BROODY FOR A FEW DAYS AFTER THAT TALK WITH DANIEL. Seeing him again in the café reawakened the resentment and anger I'd carried inside for all the years. Yet I had an understanding that this dying man was not the Daniel who had betrayed me, any more than I was the naive girl who thought love could win out over everything. I hung moodily around the farm on my time off over the next few weeks. I even fed the hens and milked a cow now and again. Da continued to weed and control pests in the kitchen garden and even Mam thawed out about my working with Daniel. I tried to put the past away again as best I could, but some hard, rough thing settled in me like a thorn, and I squirmed away from it and came back to worry it in turn.

5

"HEAVENS, WE SHOULD HAVE COME IN FIRST THING," MAM SAID.
"The cakes will taste of smoke by now."

We were in Peggy O'Shea's café for a cuppa after our grocery shopping one Friday morning. Cups and saucers rattled among the voices and the air was thick with cigarette smoke. Peggy found us a table at the back.

"How's the new job going?" Peggy asked after we'd ordered.

"Grand. It's grand."

"A nice house, is it? I hear it's the lap of luxury."

"Yes, it's very nice. But quiet, you know."

"Ah, yes, it would be. And is he keeping well? I saw him walking out the road last week. God help us, didn't he look frail? We're all sad at the news, you know."

"I'm sure you are."

"I suppose the daughter will be along any day now. From Canada, is it?"

It was always tricky to handle the natural curiosity of people and the confidentiality of my patients. The village was a world of its own, everyone knew everyone else and felt entitled to the details of their lives.

"Peggy, I've no idea really. That's Mr. Wolfe's private business. We don't really discuss his family."

Peggy's shoulders squared, and she gave the table a vicious swipe.

"My tongue is dried up, Peggy," Mam said. "I'd love one of your nice hot cuppas. And an apple slice. They're fresh, aren't they?"

"Indeed they are, Mrs. Buckley. I'll be right with you."

She stalked off without waiting to hear what I wanted.

"Nosey," Mam said. "She's always been like that. I suppose having gossip to pass along helps her business."

She leaned forward and said quietly, "*Is* the daughter coming?"

"Mam, you're as bad as she is."

Mam laughed.

⟁

"SHE MIGHT NOT COME, DELIA, BUT I NEEDED TO ASK HER," Daniel told me as we sat out in the late spring sunshine, wrapped in our coats against the cold.

It was on the tip of my tongue to add that he was a dying man and Jude would come, but I didn't. He freely acknowledged that himself in speech, but I'd learned over the years that it can be very different when someone else says it aloud. The last couple of weeks, as we sat together in the afternoons as the weather warmed, the rhododendron put out buds and the birds cheeped and twittered in the trees and bushes, I'd softened to him. Oh, I had not softened to our history, but my compassion for him rose, as it would for anyone in his position. He was visibly going downhill, which I think was, in part, due as much to the bad news of his latest tests as to his actual health. My duties had turned more to nursing in the last week, a role I was much more comfortable in.

Perhaps it was our talk about the past that made me relent. Or maybe it was Mike's joining us now and again that made me relax. Mike worked on Daniel's land a few days a week. I knew him well because as an arborist he looked after the trees on our farm and had such a sunny and easygoing disposition that I thought of him as a lad, rightly or wrongly. Sometimes in the afternoons the three of us would have tea overlooking the garden. Today it was just the two of us, Daniel and me.

"Surely she'll come. You're her father."

"She hasn't forgiven me for having Fran declared dead," he said. "But I had to do it. For Jude's sake as much as anything. I thought it'd get her over her obsession with searching, but I don't know, I think it simply made her angry with me."

"You had her declared dead?"

All the ease I'd felt a moment before vanished. I didn't want to talk about Fran's disappearance, which happened about six months after her mother died. I was away in Wales then and full of my own troubles.

"Yes, about five years ago. With no body, what could I do? Life had to go on, Delia. If anything happened to me, the estate would be in turmoil."

I sat and digested that news. It had never occurred to me that a person could just be declared dead.

"It was all such a terrible time, you know. Jude was out of her mind with worry. I got a private detective to search but nothing came up except that she took the train to Dublin the day she went missing. Jude spent years putting ads in the papers. She got her own private eye too. I thought we could put it all behind us, but that didn't work. Jude hardly speaks to me now."

"But she'll come, surely, in the circumstances? She said she would."

"I don't know that she will until she's here. We'll have to wait and see."

The prospect of Jude's arrival filled me with apprehension. An unhappy, conflicted daughter could make life very difficult up at the Big House. Nor did I want to be embroiled in any way in tensions surrounding their family history. Dealing with my own past involvement was enough. On the bright side, though, it could free me from being a companion to him. Whether or not his daughter took over that role, I would not need to spend so much time at the house in the coming weeks. Yet the prospect of her arrival stirred anxiety in me and made me question again the wisdom of my decision to involve myself once again with the Wolfe family.

6

MRS. CONWAY HAD AIRED JUDE'S OLD ROOM AND MADE UP THE bed, even though Jude wasn't due to arrive until the following week. I'd searched out a vase and had just put it on the chest of drawers intending to fill it with flowers the day she was due when the doorbell clanged through the house. I pulled off my apron and patted my hair in place in the hall mirror before opening the door.

"Yes?" I said to the woman on the step. She had a large suitcase and wore a blue wool coat way too heavy for the warm May day.

"Hello, I'm Jude. Daniel's daughter. "

She looked nothing like the young woman in the wedding photo. She looked nothing like Daniel or her sister, Fran, either. Fran had been athletic, with a halo of frizzy red hair. Jude was dark-haired and slight, but she had her mother's eyes.

"Oh, come in, come in."

She hesitated on the step, turned to look back down the driveway, then stepped over the sill.

"We weren't expecting you until next week. You should have let us know. How did you get out here?"

I covered my fluster with a flurry of questions. She found a spot for her suitcase in the hall and hung her coat on the coat tree.

"Sorry, I know. Sorry. I hope it's all right. I got an earlier flight. Once I decided to come, I wanted to get here as soon as I could."

About to show her into the parlour, I stopped. She'd know her way around this house better than I did. I introduced myself as Daniel's nurse.

"Daniel is resting now. I'll bring you tea; you must be exhausted. And famished. I'll bring you a cup of tea and a bite to eat. Or would you prefer coffee?"

"Thanks. I'll come into the kitchen with you. A cup of tea would be great."

I tried to get the measure of her as I put on the kettle and set out cups and saucers. She looked older than I had thought she would, although she was probably exhausted from the trip. What was she now? About thirty-eight or -nine? She looked nothing like her sister, for which I was grateful, though she still had that quiet, watchful air I remembered about her from years ago.

"How is he?" she asked as she sipped her tea.

"For now he's not too bad. Things are progressing a bit faster than we hoped initially."

I slipped into my professional role and relaxed. She seemed nice enough. A straightforward sort of person, who didn't at all remember me from her youth. And why should she? We'd never socialized, moving as we did in very different circles.

"You'll want to rest. Daniel won't be up for a while, unless the door woke him. Your old room is ready. Or at least Daniel said it was your old room. I'd have put flowers in for you today if I'd known..."

I let the rest trail away, worried I'd sound offended by her early arrival.

"Oh, don't worry about a thing. I'm sorry to take everyone by surprise, but..." She shrugged.

When I had the place to myself again I tidied up and breathed a sigh of relief. Just as well she had arrived unexpectedly; at least Daniel wouldn't have time to get all tense about it. He'd been fussing about getting to the airport to greet her. That was when he wasn't fretting she'd change her mind. I set off to the village and left them privacy for their meeting.

☙

THOSE FIRST DAYS AND WEEKS SHE PROWLED THE HOUSE AND
grounds like a cat marking territory. She called her father by his
name instead of Dad, or Daddy, or even Father. She sought out
Mike, and when Daniel was resting she was out shadowing him at
his work on the grounds. As a result he didn't join Daniel and me
for tea in the afternoon quite as much. It was especially nice outside
now that summer was coming in. The backyard was full of birdsong.
Daniel had me naming the birds we heard and he was getting quite
good at identifying them. Most afternoons Jude joined us. Daniel
was doing his best with her, but their relationship was cool; each of
them tried too hard to stay away from touchy things. I missed what
ease there had been between Daniel, Mike and me, as I couldn't
quite relax in Jude's company. How could I have conceived of such
a thing a few months ago? Me, missing time with Daniel? The truth
was, he'd become a patient. As always, I felt a deep compassion for
the struggles people had to come to terms with their own mortality.

At one of our afternoon teas, things changed between father
and daughter. Jude poured the tea and handed around the cups.
Daniel's eyes had a bit of sparkle to them again. Only the fact that
he kept his movements to a minimum showed his energy was not
up to much. He worked on his writing less, too, but what he did
brought a weary slackness to his face these days that eased after
his rest.

"The garden is gone to wrack and ruin," Jude observed.

"Isn't Mike keeping it up? I thought he did a good job," Daniel
said.

"Oh, he does. The larger grounds are beautiful. Just the kitchen
garden. It's gone wild. Impossible to tell the difference between
the herbs and weeds anymore."

"Ah," Daniel said. "Well, I haven't been here a lot and with your
mother gone, I thought Mike had enough to do without that."

The wicker creaked as Daniel shifted in his chair. A crow took
up admonishment from the roof.

"Jude, you know I'm dying," Daniel said after he took a couple
of sips of tea.

"Yes, I know. I do know."

"You will inherit the house and land. I hope you and Matthew will live here."

"What about Fran?" she asked. "I know you've declared her dead, but what if she turns up?"

"Let's leave that aside for now. This place has been in your mother's family for generations. She wouldn't want to see it sold. That's what this is about, right now."

"I would never sell it, Daniel. You must know that. Never."

It shocked me to think that Daniel thought his daughter would sell the estate.

"It needs to be lived in, Jude. It needs life."

"Well, by your admission, it hasn't had much for quite a while. Since Mother died and Fran left. So why do you worry about that now?"

"Well, now I think that was a bit of a mistake. It needs life. Spending time here and having you and Delia around shows me that. You and Matthew can raise children here."

Jude got up and fiddled with the tea cozy, then offered us the pot. Her hand trembled as she poured into my cup.

"Matthew and I are divorced," she said when she settled herself back in her chair. "We have been for a year."

Daniel sighed. He stirred the spoon round and round, the faint scrape off the bottom of the cup and the caw of the crow the only sounds for a moment.

"I hoped you two would live here. Raise your children here. But that's not for me to say. Think about making it your home. That's all I ask."

"My life is in Canada now. That's where I live. I know nobody here. Well, now I know Delia, but not one other living soul. I never had any friends here. We were at boarding school. Besides, what would I do here?"

"You can do what you do over there. Your art. You can do it in comfort. You won't need to keep a job, Jude. You'll be well off, you know that."

"And Fran?"

"Fran is not coming back. Even you must know that by now. It is unlikely I, at any rate, will ever know what happened to her. Or you, come to that. As far as the estate is concerned, she's legally dead. It's all up to you now."

Jude frowned into her cup and remained silent. Daniel leaned across and touched her shoulder.

"Just think about it, Jude. Please. Think about it."

"I don't know how you can give up on your own daughter. I just don't know what kind of father can do that. A piece of paper does not make her dead to me."

With that statement she got up and went into the house. The crow on the roof gave one more loud caw, then flew off.

"Well," Daniel said, "that didn't go so well. She'll come round. She will. Don't you think so?"

There was no answer to this, nor did he really expect one. For all their sakes I did hope they'd make peace on the matter, but then, not everything gets resolved the way we'd like it.

"Time will tell," I said. "Time will tell."

Tension ran between the two of them all the next week, though they both made an effort at cordiality. Tension rose in me too as the shadow of the past wound around us like a cobweb, preventing us from untangling ourselves. In the month since Jude had come Daniel had lost some ground, and the walls I'd built to keep the past locked away began to crumble. In spite of my efforts to shun the memory of the end of our affair and all that happened next, it rose to my mind until I began to think that despite the financial ease my work with him produced, being in such proximity to him was wearing on me. Jude's still-raw distress at the loss of her sister was no help. As a result I didn't linger after supper, and on my next day off I went up to Dublin to see Maggie.

All the way up on the bus I was full of wondering how I would find her. The whole business with Jude and Daniel reminded me that her condition had been going on for over twenty years, which seemed unbelievable. She was my older sister, who finished her university degree the year after she left the convent, in spite of my father's grumblings. He was proud enough of her to put on his best suit and go with the rest of us to her graduation. "Where did she come from at all?" he asked a million times. She was the first of us to get a degree. She was brave, too. She stood by me during my troubles, and was to be my saviour, before everything went terribly wrong. At first it was just obsessive worry with her, then a fear of going out, then a withdrawal into some other world where she quickly lost the way back to normal. I was in Wales at the time and came back and forth as often as I could until it became clear poor Maggie couldn't cope anymore. I took it upon myself to see that she was all right, taken care of. It was the very least I could do. If I hadn't involved her in my mess perhaps she'd be healthy and happy today. This whole business between Daniel and Jude stirred me up, so a visit became urgent for me. I needed to see that she was as all right as it was possible for her to be.

As the past was so much on my mind, I had somehow expected a change in Maggie one way or the other. She was no better or worse than ever. She chattered no more nor less than usual and only asked me once if it was stormy out, but it was more a matter of conversation than the fearful dread with which she often asked me. She had a terrible fear of storms altogether. As I sat and she turned the pages of a magazine she never actually read, my agitation built. Bitter regret at my own part in how things turned out, and a renewed resentment of Daniel. I'd tried to make amends for my mistakes by taking on the care of the dying, and the irony of taking care of Daniel Wolfe made my head spin. For once I was eager to get away from Maggie, but home and Kiltilly didn't seem such a refuge anymore.

7

DANIEL SPENT THE MORNING FRETTING ABOUT JUDE AND
the estate. He wanted some assurance from her that she'd make
the estate her home. I could have pointed out he'd hardly done
that himself, but, determined to keep out of it all, I took off for
Peggy's and a bit of peace and quiet as soon as he went for his
afternoon rest. Barely was my tea in front of me than Jude came
in. She'd found an old bicycle in the shed out back and spent days
cleaning, oiling and getting new tires for it. Now she took off
every day for a ride, and here she was all red-cheeked with a light
sheen of sweat on her forehead. I would have preferred my own
company just then, but I couldn't let her sit alone so I invited her
to join me. Far from the spoiled daughter I had expected, she was
very natural and basically a kind person, which she showed often
in her care for Daniel, despite their differences.

"How're you settling in?" I asked her.

"Oh, fine. Fine. You know, it's strange being back. I haven't
been here for about fifteen years. It's sure changed. More
prosperous than I remember. And more modern. Look at this
café."

She was right. Change had arrived quickly with the prosperity
of the 1980s.

"It's still a small Irish village at heart, make no mistake," I
said.

I was thinking about how gossip could still ruin reputations,
although it seemed that the youngsters these days didn't care at
all what was said about them.

"Yes, I like that it's small and personal. I forgot what a place like this was. People ask after Daniel when I go into shops. It's good."

I smeared a piece of cream on my apple crumble and said nothing. She had either forgotten that the village had another, less charitable side. Or perhaps she was insulated against it by money and position. Whenever it got too close here, the likes of her could take off for a while to live somewhere else, escape the wagging tongues.

"Lots of visitors come out here now for a holiday. I don't remember that."

It was true. The harbour had been done up with a walking trail and the woods up on the hill at the north end of the village had a lovely lake that the county council had decided to exploit. It was a mixed blessing for Kiltilly. It brought prosperity but it also brought a restlessness to the youngsters. They were all eager for the cities now, rather than seeing it as a necessary migration as they did in my day. They had no interest in the local drama group and only went to the small local cinema in the bad winter weather, preferring to drink at the overhauled local pub if they stayed in the village. When I had to leave here for months in Wales I thought my heart would break. Away, I missed the farm, my parents, the soft turf-scented air. Nice as it was, Cardiff stifled me, although the circumstances I was in then didn't help.

"The weekends are wicked. You can't get in the door here then," is all I said.

"It is strange being here, you know. It brings the past back. Mother's death, Fran's disappearance, it all seems so fresh again. To tell the truth, I find it a bit hard. Last week in the village I heard someone laugh and she sounded exactly like Fran. I can't quite believe Daniel is so ready to believe she won't ever come back."

Fran wouldn't ever come back. That was the truth, but I wasn't going to have that discussion with Jude here and now. Never, really.

"It's best to leave the past behind you."

"So you keep saying. But it's not so easy to do, is it?"

No, it wasn't. If anyone should know that it was me. I'd done a good job of living in the here and now so far, yet these last few weeks I wondered if I could bear to work out my time with Daniel. The family's pain at Fran's loss was hard to bear. I'd not thought much about how the family coped with it, as I'd been away and my own desperation, my bitterness with Daniel, overshadowed everything. Maggie was going off the rails then too.

"No, it's not easy to lose someone," was all I said, as my own losses rose in my throat and blocked out any words of comfort I might have offered. The more time I spent with Jude and Daniel, the more whatever peace I'd gained over the years faded. I reminded myself that I was doing all of this for Maggie. Mam and Da too, but mostly for Maggie. One thing I was sure of: no matter the grief and anguish of the Wolfe family, my first responsibility was to protect my own. Once I'd believed in honour and love, but I'd learned my lesson. I owed nothing to the Wolfe family. Whatever guilt I carried I would deal with, I could bear.

8

AT THREE O'CLOCK MOST DAYS JUDE WENT OFF ON HER bicycle and Daniel gave in to fatigue. Each day he worked on his book for a couple of hours, then insisted on putting on a show for Jude, stayed up too long, talked too much, but he wasn't really fooling anyone. Jude was clear about his condition, but she indulged him as best she could. She hadn't brought up the issue of her sister lately, so although their relationship was not warm, it was smooth enough. They both pretended he was in better health than he was. Jude's way of seeing he got rest was to go out on her own every day after the midday meal. Perhaps it restored her as well. She'd take off on her bicycle for hours. Once I asked her where she spent so much time.

"There's a hill back of the road that overlooks the village. I used to go there with a book on fine days after Fran left for university and I was here alone. From there I can see the village laid out below."

A small possessive resentment rose in me. That was my spot, mine and Maggie's. I could hardly bear that it was hers too. Ridiculous, I knew, so I tried to let it go.

This high summer day after the cheery *tring-tring* of Jude's bike bell died away, I helped Daniel upstairs to his room. A week ago he had been able to make it himself, but now he was so weak and slow I hovered behind him ready to steady him if necessary as he mounted the steps.

I helped him undress. So many hollows and bones on him. As I eased his shirt off his shoulders I remembered other days when I had undressed him, the delicious pleasure of paring him down to nakedness, my body's throb in anticipation of what was to come. The memory took me by surprise. Earlier the two of us had been watching Jude and Mike chat by the old kitchen garden. As we watched she flicked something off his shoulder. Mike reached one arm up to a tree branch, perfectly posed to show off his body, strong from all the physical work he did. As a shaft of sunlight caught the two of them, picked up the soft flirt in Jude's posture and the answer in Mike's, I yearned for love. There had been a few fellows I'd walked out with over the years, but my responsibility for Maggie, together with my general lack of trust after Daniel ended things with me, kept me my own woman.

Daniel sighed beside me.

"They seem friendly," Daniel said. "Maybe they'll make a match. What do you think?" he asked.

I didn't hold out much hope for a permanent match between these two, as I had no confidence they could bridge the social difference between them.

"Maybe they will. Maybe they won't," I answered.

BY A QUARTER TO FOUR DANIEL WAS ASLEEP. INSTEAD OF TIDYING up or going into the village as usual, I sat at the kitchen table, hands clasped on the polished surface. It was the longest day of the year, a day that made me melancholy, turn in on myself. Thinking on the past yields nothing at all, but I kept this one ritual day to remember and mourn. All the people I'd seen through the door to eternity, from the newborns to the very old, were on my mind. I chose to work with the dying as reparation for my sins, to be present for the very moment a soul passes into the hands of God and to offer what comfort I could. Afterwards is for the living. They experience the loss, the relief, the guilt for the past, but that is not my concern. My part is done. This year another burden was added to my reflections, such as they were. I would soon see Daniel

Wolfe through that door, the man I'd resented for so long, and the one who had now saved me, Maggie and the farm. I watched the sun creep across the room and spotlight random things, the edge of the countertop, the glass jug of flowers I forgot to put back on the table when I cleared it after our meal. The light moved to the head of the table and hit the old wooden chair. The oak worn smooth as river stones from the rub of Daniel's back was ghostly through the dust motes in the sun's rays. The room dimmed as the sun sank behind the tall pine at the west edge of the herb garden in the backyard. I jumped when the brassy chime of the doorbell rang, shuffled off my slippers and stuffed my feet into my court shoes. The heels tapped a smart tattoo on the wooden floor to the front door.

The young woman on the doorstep looked ordinary enough, brown hair cut a bit unfashionably short. She wore a cornflower blue T-shirt, jeans and heavy laced boots out of keeping with a mild summer day. Her T-shirt exactly matched the colour of her eyes. My heart went crosswise in my chest because I recognized who she was. There was no mistaking those eyes. Perhaps if she had shown up at any other time, or even any other place except Daniel Wolfe's doorstep, I would have reacted differently. I hope I would have. Instead I gave her my most formal face.

"Yes?"

"Hi, are you Delia Buckley?" she asked.

I thought about denying it, but if someone from the village had already told the girl where to find me there was no point in it.

"I am."

"My name is Iris Butler. I'm trying to find my family. They came from these parts, and I think...hope...you can help me."

She spoke slowly to offset the rolling 'r's and lilt of her Scottish accent. I heard the quick intake of breath; saw the quick flash of tongue that slid over Iris Butler's lips as she prepared to speak again. I cut her off, anxious to get her on her way before Jude arrived back.

"I don't know any Butlers hereabouts."

"Yes, I know. Look, may I come in and explain? It's a long shot, I know, but maybe you can help. Really, this is my last hope."

I fought the impulse to slam the door on her. Before I had time to think of something to cut her off the *tring-tring* of the bicycle bell rang out to announce Jude's return. Iris turned toward the sound and the two of us watched Jude emerge round the bend in the drive. She drew level with us and hopped off her bike. As soon as she heard it was a search for family I knew there'd be no getting rid of this Iris Butler.

"Oh, Delia," she said. "We have a visitor. How nice."

Left with no choice, I introduced them. Iris walked down and held out a hand to shake with Jude.

"Sorry to barge in," she said. "I'm on a quest to find some family my mother told me was in this region. I think, well, I hope Delia can help me."

Jude, of course, invited her in for tea. Just as Iris Butler lifted her foot over the sill I decided that I would give her no help at all. She could find her family on her own. Let sleeping dogs lie, that was the old adage, and by God that's what I vowed to do. But the dog was already on its feet, I would discover in the days that followed. Iris Butler walked through the door and brought the past with her.

&

WHILE JUDE MADE TEA IN THE KITCHEN, IRIS AND I SAT IN THE parlour, listening to the rattle of cups onto saucers and the clink of spoons. I took the chair next to the fireplace. She perched on one end of the settee, her feet neatly together on the shag rug, her head swivelling right and left as she took in the room. Her eyes lingered on the row of photographs along the mantel.

"It must be brilliant to work for Mr. Wolfe," she said.

"It suits me well enough."

"I read all his books as a kid. My mother started reading them to me when I was tiny. I loved them. I'm sorry to hear he's so ill."

She was cut off by Jude's arrival with a tray full of tea trappings. Iris jumped up to help.

"No need, really." Jude waved her away and set the tray down on the coffee table, an oval glass-topped affair, edged in dark wood that showed every fingerprint and crumb.

"So," Jude said as soon as we'd settled the tea pouring. "What makes you think we can help you find your family?"

"Maybe you can't, really. I don't know. My mother died six months ago. She got sick quite suddenly. Lung cancer. She wasn't able to talk much at the end. After Sam, that's my adopted father, died, it was always just the two of us. I didn't think I had any other family at all. Mum said we didn't. The last day she was able to speak at all she said I should go find my family. At first I thought she just meant I should, you know, make a life for myself. Her speech was slurred and voice was weak and very hard to hear. She grabbed my arm. *Find them*, she said. I heard that clearly and realized what she wanted. I asked her *who, find who?* She clearly said *your aunties, your granny*. Most of her strength left her then and she slurred something like Kiltilly and Buckley, but it could have been Butler and Kilty, really, and I'm beginning to wonder if I've been mistaken about what she said at all. I've found four Buckley families in towns that sound like Kiltilly. None of them were connected to Mum in any way. Then I met a guy in a pub in Scotland a few months ago and he said he knew Buckleys in the town of Kiltilly, so here I am."

She turned to me.

"You're my last hope, really. There are no more Buckleys that I can find in towns that sound like Kiltilly. I would so like to meet family. All my life it's just been Mum and me. No aunts. No uncles. No granny or granddad. It would be so very cool to find someone, anyone, related to me. Anyone at all."

9

"MY MUM NEVER LIED TO ME, I WAS SURE OF THAT. SHE NEVER lied. But on her deathbed she either told the biggest lie of all, or made a lie of my whole life."

Iris's eyes got teary as she began her tale. It was hard not to have sympathy for her. I did, I felt it. There was a lot I could have told her then, but my reawakened memories of Daniel's betrayal and my own losses blocked the words in my throat. Through the years I'd worked hard to earn trust as a nurse and make a place for myself in the life of the village. Kiltilly had moved into the modern age in many ways, but it still held onto the old-fashioned mores. Besides, I couldn't risk that Daniel would find a way to change his mind about giving me the farm. Nonetheless, I listened carefully to Iris Butler's story.

Iris and her mother lived alone together after her stepfather, Sam, was killed in a motorcycle accident when she was seven. Her mother, Maggie Butler, and Sam had been together since Iris was a baby, though they'd never married.

"He didn't die right away, but Mum was straight with me about how badly injured he was. She told me he wasn't likely to live. She hid nothing," Iris said. "She told me we're all going to die. We just know Sam will die very soon."

He died, she said, three days, six hours and twenty-five minutes later. He left them a life insurance policy which they used to buy a cottage.

It was a small place, no more than a bedroom, a big kitchen and living room warmed by a huge range.

"It was our castle. We got a sign made for the gate that said "Little House." Iris dabbed her eyes with a ragged paper hankie. "We planned out the garden all winter and planted it in the spring. In the months after Mum died I couldn't bear to be in that house. Every Friday after work I'd drive out into the countryside, find some wild, deserted places and walk until my legs ached. I'd choose a spot high on the edge of some hill or mountain, take out my flask of tea and bag of sandwiches and fruit. When I was tired I lay down on the grass and heather and slept. But as much as I found comfort in those wild places, I couldn't tend the little garden. The beds are overrun with weeds, the cabbages and herbs gone to seed. It went back to the wilds as well."

"I'm so sorry, Iris," Jude said. "It's so hard to lose family. I know it. When I was sixteen, my mother died."

Iris nodded. She tried to blow her nose again but the tissue was used and useless. I passed her a box from the side table.

"What makes you think I know anything about your family?" I asked her.

"It was what she said just before she died. When I was a wee thing I always asked her where I came from. The story she told me was always the same.

"She said it had been cold all day. The light dawned late and left early and by the morning a few flakes of snow skidded around the house. The curtains in the kitchen of the tiny flat she lived in were grimy from the open windows of summer and autumn, so Mum decided it was a good day to wash them. She wanted them clean and bright to entice inside whatever dim light there was to welcome me.

"As she emptied the soapy water out of the big washbasin, she felt the first twinge. Maybe today is the day, she thought. Maybe my baby will come today. She had thought that a few days earlier when she'd had a twinge, and every day for the last three days, but every morning she woke up and was still Mum-in-waiting. So she filled the basin with rinse water, rinsed the curtains, wrung them out, and shook the big wrinkles out of them. She opened the brand new clothes-drying rack and put it in the bathtub. As she spread the curtains on the drying rack she got a big twinge. It was a no-nonsense one. She called her friend Annie, who came right away and took her to the hospital. By teatime, I had arrived. I was pink and soft. She knew right away my name was Iris, because it means Rainbow, or bringer of joy.

"That's the story she told me. It was a lie. I asked Annie, Mum's best friend, if the story was true and she said she only met Mum when I was about three months old. I used to ask about my real father, and Mum said he didn't matter. We only had each other as family. Just the two of us and Sam."

She searched first my face, then Jude's, as if we could solve this mystery. Jude patted her arm. Iris sighed and took up the tale again.

"You see, I searched everywhere for a town with a name similar to what I thought she said. When I got here I was certain I was right, because we have a picture on the wall at home, a little watercolour, of this very village. I recognized it immediately. When I asked in the village about Buckley, I was told you were here. Your family is the only Buckley left in Kiltilly who could possibly be related to me."

"How old are you now? Did your mother live here then?" I asked.

"I'm twenty-two. I was born in June 1968, in Scotland"

"There you are," I said. "It's not me at all you're looking for. I'm sorry, Iris, but I think you have had a trip for nothing. My cousins are all married women and accounted for since then."

"What about brothers? Maybe one is her father," Jude said.

"I don't have brothers, Jude. It was just my sister Maggie and me. I'm sorry, but we are not your family."

"I'm not even sure I was born in Scotland. When I went to search for my long-form birth certificate, it didn't exist in the Scottish registry. I don't know how I got the short-form one, but that's all I have."

It was on the tip of my tongue so say something then, but before I could Jude broke in.

"Oh dear, Iris," she said. "You have a real riddle on your hands. I'd love to hear more of your story. Why don't you come tomorrow for lunch? You can meet my father. He'll be glad of a new face around here. Perhaps we can figure something out about where to look next between us. Can't we, Delia?"

10

I WOULD HAVE GIVEN A GREAT DEAL TO GET OUT OF LUNCH, BUT I needed to be at the Big House to get Daniel ready for the day. He stayed in bed until mid-morning now and spent precious little time on his book. He was still determined to finish it, but it was more intention than action recently. To be fair, he was in a lot of pain and on a punishing daily regimen of drugs. His energy was failing visibly.

The prospect of a visitor energized him, though. He brightened up and gave instructions on what to serve for lunch, including a bottle of wine.

"I don't know why you asked her to come. Sure we're no help to her at all," I said to Jude as she was flitting about preparing lunch. Daniel supervised from his chair at the head of the kitchen table. My tone was sharper than I intended. I hadn't slept much the night before, unsettled by Iris and her story.

"She's feeling a bit lost. Her mother is recently dead and she's trying to honour her wishes. To find family now would be great for her. The poor thing could do with a bit of support," Jude answered.

"She's grasping at straws, that's what she is."

"It will be fine, Delia," Daniel said. "No need to make a fuss. A young person around for lunch will liven us all up."

"She's just holding on to deathbed ravings. Best not to encourage her."

"That sounds so cold, Delia," Jude said. "She must have family somewhere. Why not look for them with what clues she has?"

I remembered what Daniel had said about Jude's search for her sister after she went missing, so I said no more.

The doorbell rang at almost exactly at 12.30 p.m. Jude ushered Iris in to meet Daniel.

"It's so nice to meet you, Mr. Wolfe. An honour, really. All the kids in Scotland read your books. Including me."

Daniel looked confused for a moment and left her hand hanging in air.

"Daniel?" Jude nudged him.

"Ah, yes, thank you. So nice to meet you."

He pumped her arm until Jude broke in and led us into the dining room. He couldn't keep his eyes off Iris, and I fancied I could see his mind ticking away. Perhaps he saw in her what I saw myself.

Daniel was at his most charming over lunch. He quizzed Iris about her mother, but Iris didn't have much to add to what she'd already told Jude and me the day before, except that her mother had trained as a surgical nurse.

"I didn't know that. I found her documents after she died," she told us.

"Ah, Delia, did you ever come across her? If she came from these parts, maybe she trained with you," Daniel asked me.

Flustered, I let my fork clatter to the floor. Jude jumped up to get me another.

"No, not that I can think of. She was younger than me, so we wouldn't necessarily know each other. Did she nurse in Scotland?" I asked Iris.

"No. She worked in a bank as long as I can remember."

"And Butler is her own name, is that right?" Daniel asked. Iris confirmed that it was, as far as she knew. Daniel sipped his wine and lapsed into silence.

"It's a lovely house, Mr. Wolfe," Iris said after a moment. The conversation turned to the history of the estate, much to my relief. I looked around the room, trying to see it through Iris's eyes. I was accustomed to the absence of ordinary things I took for granted in my own house and the houses of friends. No Sacred Heart lamp to be seen, no religious pictures, no crucifixes on the wall. I had become so used to the lack of a holy water font by the front door that I was forgetting to dip my fingers and bless myself in my own home. I wondered if Iris was Catholic, but I didn't ask her.

As soon as lunch was cleared Daniel invited Iris on a tour of the house and grounds.

"Come with us, Jude," he said. "And you too, Delia. You haven't had a formal tour of the place yet, have you?"

"I'll join you outside when you're ready," I said, knowing he'd need someone to lean on. He wanted to interest Jude in the property, and couldn't pass up the opportunity Iris's presence gave. So far Jude had resisted all his efforts, except for spending time with Mike. Most of their time was spent while he worked, so I supposed she was learning something about running the place, and didn't want to let Daniel know that yet. Or maybe they were falling in love. Whatever it was, Jude wasn't talking about it. While the three of them toured the ground floor, I got a warm jacket for Daniel and sat on one of the rattan chairs out back to wait.

Through the open window I could hear him talking about the house. It had a long history in the hands of the FitzGibbons, and the thought that Daniel and I could have lived here with our child came to mind, but with some effort I dismissed it. No use at all thinking about that. The Big House had never been a consideration of mine then, but now a new bitterness at Daniel clattered in my heart.

As we walked out on one of the trails through the woods, Daniel held my arm and Jude and Iris followed. He surprised me by knowing the names of most of the trees and much of their history on the land. We moved slowly and he leaned more heavily on my arm by the time we reached the bench under the elm about halfway across this part of the estate.

"My sister Fran and I used to play here," Jude said to Iris. "It was our favourite place. Sometimes I'd come here alone with a book and our little cat, Skin. We buried him just behind the tree a few yards in. Come, I'll show you."

"Is that your sister in the photos in the parlour? Is she away?"

Daniel sat heavily on the wooden bench. His face shone with sweat, which was not altogether due to the warm day.

"She just vanished one day. She told me she was going away for a few days, and that's the last anyone saw her. It was years ago. I still miss her," she told Iris.

"You never found out what happened to her? Oh, that's so awful."

"Thanks," Jude said and turned the conversation. "Look, Mike has kept the grave all neat. You'll have to meet him."

They went to the big pine to look at the little cat grave. Daniel and I sat and listened to them chatter. It was quite a warm day and a spread of branches over the bench cast a dappled shade.

"I hope this visit doesn't work her up about Fran again," I said to Daniel.

Before he could answer the two of them returned. He patted the seat beside him. Iris sat and turned her face up to the sun. Jude paced behind the bench.

"Come, Jude, sit with us." Daniel inched over to make room for her. Jude sat.

"Skin's grave is still intact," she said.

Daniel shrugged. "That cat was the bane of my life. Mike Kennedy's a good man. He cleared up the cat's grave, but said the cross was rotted out. Can't think what you girls put up a cross for."

"Fran didn't think it was necessary, but I wanted it," Jude said. "Can't remember why now. We buried a few mice here too. Skin's murders, we called them."

"Did you have other animals? Do you have a whole pet cemetery here somewhere?" Iris looked around as if one would pop up among the trees.

"No, we just had that one cat, though it seemed like a hundred." Daniel laughed. "I think it had a grudge against me."

"I thought your house would be full of animals. You have some great ones in your books."

"That's where I liked them best. They didn't run away with my stuff and eat it."

I listened to them banter. Iris told stories about some of the pets she'd had. Daniel listened and asked questions as if this conversation were the most important in the world. As Iris and he conversed, he laughed more than I'd heard him do so far.

The walk back to the house was slower, and Daniel stumbled now and again on the uneven ground.

"Careful," Jude said after one such stumble. She came forward to take his other arm. The path was so narrow that it was even harder to walk this way, so she dropped back again to walk with Iris.

We settled into the chairs by the garden. Daniel was out of breath and sat heavily, but insisted on tea, or whiskey for those who wanted it. Jude and I had tea, Daniel and Iris a whiskey.

"So, you're looking for your mother's family," he said to Iris as he swirled the ice in his drink.

"Yes. I have some photos, if you want to see her," Iris said. "And I brought the little watercolour of the village that hung on our wall."

She went inside and came back with a brown envelope. I watched her open it, glad no one could hear my heart rattle about in my chest. She pulled out the watercolour first, then two small square photos with serrated edges from the envelope. She passed me the watercolour. It showed the village from the square near the war memorial. The old TB hospital was on the hill above the village, still a hospital then, and the building that now housed the café, a small variety store and a craft shop was still part of the old Garda barracks. The road to Daniel's house led away to one side. It was a shock to see it, because, even though it was unsigned, I knew at once that my sister Maggie had painted it. She was a dab hand at watercolours when she was younger. She sold them to raise money for the church at the Christmas sale. I passed the little picture to Daniel without a word. He looked at it briefly, then passed it on to Jude.

"Let me see those, then," I said to Iris and held out my hand for the photos.

"I don't have many photos of her. She hated having her picture taken," Iris said. "When I went through them after she died these two were the best we had."

No matter how I tilted and turned the snaps in the light, I didn't learn much from them about Iris's mother. The first picture was of two females, one clearly a younger version of Iris. The other woman was about five foot four or five, a bit taller than Iris today. She was very thin; her head was turned to the side and was wrapped in a scarf that trailed down across her left shoulder. All I could see was the line of her jaw and cheekbone on the right side of her face, the rest no more than a blurry shadow.

The second picture showed what could have been the same person. She stood full face to the camera, but the photo was out of focus. She wore a wide-shouldered jacket and midi, her legs cut off at the ankles in the photo. She stood in front of some impressive stone building, her hat pulled low on her forehead. She could be any trendy woman of her day.

"Can't say I know her," I said.

I held out the photo to Jude.

The eagerness in Jude as she took the photos roused pity in me, for at once I realized she was hoping against all hope that it might be her lost sister. Her shoulders drooped and some of the light left her face after she'd examined them as closely as I had done. God forgive me, I should have been more sympathetic to her still mourning the loss of her sister, to her hope that Fran would turn up one day. She needed to put it behind her and move on. We all have to do it with the tragedies and disappointments of our lives. Few of us get the outcomes we want when it comes right down to it.

11

DANIEL WAS BESOTTED WITH IRIS. HE LIT UP LIKE AN ALTAR whenever she showed up. I should have been happy that something cheered him up, the state he was in, but I couldn't help but wish it were not Iris who caused it. Ever since Jude had invited her to lunch she'd become a regular visitor. It seemed, in fact, that she was everywhere, all the time. On a trip to the butcher's the other day I saw her run past the window dressed in a pair of shorts and T-shirt. Her legs pumped up and down with no apparent effort as she loped along. She ran every day, she told me later, and it showed, because although she moved with some speed, it looked like it was no effort for her at all. It was a long time since I felt my own body light, breath that slipped in and out with ease. A weight was on me these days, underscored by the silences that fell on the little groups of villagers as I drew near on the street or in the café. Even outside the Chapel on Sunday. They were all speculating about Iris showing up looking for her family, the Buckleys. I wished her gone back to where she came from. Speedily.

She was underfoot at Daniel's more often than not. At first it was Jude who asked her up to the house. They had a mutual interest in the gardening and I thought perhaps Jude was lonely with no young people around except for Mike. Then Daniel took a shine to her and wore himself out as they played poker in the afternoons. In no time at all she was a daily visitor.

Any fine day found Jude and Iris out in the garden, and this day was no exception. They dug and weeded what was once the kitchen garden and already had a few piles of discarded plants on the side of the path. From the kitchen window I watched Jude on her haunches as she pulled weeds from between the rosemary and oregano and tossed them to the edge of the path. Iris dug out the old potato plants that had gone to seed. She bent and lifted the shovel, came up with a sod of earth attached to old plants, her muscles bunching and flexing with each load.

And to think that I was the one who suggested the garden needed attention in an effort to find something to occupy Jude! Well, I never imagined Iris Butler showing up when I did that.

Jude and Iris laughed at something. They stood close together, Iris leaning on the spade as she bent over in mirth, their giggles almost indistinguishable from each other's.

"Iris brings a bit of life to this place, doesn't she? She cheers me up, and Jude too."

I jumped out of my skin when Daniel spoke. So absorbed was I in the two women, I hadn't heard him come in. We stood a moment together observing them.

"Aye, she does that. I hope Jude isn't getting any strange notions," he said.

"What do you mean? What sort of notions?"

"That this is Fran's child. You know she's thinking it, same as I know it. Are you sure you're not related to her some way? By a cousin or something?"

For a moment I wondered if he was playing with me. It was hard to believe he did not see what I saw when I looked at her. Before I could answer, Iris looked towards us and waved. Daniel waved back.

"She cheers the place up, though, doesn't she?" he said again, then took up his walking sticks and went out to them.

"IRIS IS A GREAT HELP CLEARING THAT PATCH. SHE KNOWS WEEDS from useful plants, which is more than I can say of myself."

Jude and I were in the kitchen after Iris left and Daniel went up to rest. I sorted out his medications so that Jude could keep them straight the next day when I was off.

"You're making good progress there, all right," I said.

"Yes, thank heaven. For a while it seemed like we were getting nowhere. You know, Iris had all her hope on you being able to help with her search for family. Too bad you can't."

"Well, she got on this long without them, it seems to me she'll do all right on her own. She's looking for a needle in a haystack."

I counted the pills, then double-checked them in the little squares of the box Jude used when I wasn't here.

"I can understand it. I'll have no real family left when Daniel dies. He has a sister, Aunt Maud. She's older than him and is crippled with arthritis. She lives in New Zealand and never married. Mother was an only child, so unless Fran turns up, it's just me."

"You can't possibly believe your sister will show up after all this time, can you?"

I was genuinely curious, and my question brought tears to her eyes. She sniffled, got a hankie from her skirt pocket and blew her nose.

"It's my hope, Delia. I just can't give up hope. It seems like letting her down, giving up on her. So many times over the years, walking in a street somewhere or at an event, I have imagined I caught a glimpse of her, or heard her laugh. Many times I've followed some strange woman in the street, convinced by her walk, or her hair, or even some gesture she made, a turn of the head or some other thing, that she was Fran. Even when I knew the person I followed was too young I still followed them. For a few years I kept a second job so I could pay a private investigator to look for her. The PI had no more success than I."

She wiped her nose again. I snapped the lid on the pillbox shut and patted her on the shoulder.

"I'm so sorry, Jude. But you know…"

"Yes," she interrupted me, "it's better to let the past go. So you keep saying, but it's not such an easy thing to do, is it?"

"No, pet, it isn't. Not at all," I said. "But we have to sometimes. We just have to."

⟁

AROUND THIS TIME I SAW A SOFTENING IN JUDE TOWARD DANIEL. Perhaps in the evenings when I had gone home they had time to talk. Daniel no longer sent her so many long, broody looks when he thought she didn't notice.

"You seem to have forgiven your father," I said to her one afternoon when we were alone. She looked at me in surprise.

"It seems I have. I suppose so. He's so frail, Delia. Whatever grudges I have kept against him seem...trivial...in the face of his life ending."

She echoed what I'd been thinking myself. All those years I'd nursed a hatred and contempt of him seemed a waste of time now. Besides, they'd had no impact on him, only on me.

"Compassion is a good thing," I said, as much to myself as to Jude.

She nodded and looked at the floor. A tear took a slow trip down the side of her nose. I gathered her in my arms and patted her back. She clung to me like a child as her shoulders shook with grief. Something inside me shifted, dislocated, as I held Daniel and Ellen Wolfe's surviving daughter and tried to console her.

12

ST. JOSEPH'S CHURCH WAS AT THE FAR END OF THE
village from Daniel's place. As I walked in for Devotions on
Friday the soft misty rain was more like a caress than a nuisance.
By the time I reached the middle of Main Street I had joined up
with the other people as they made their way to the chapel. It
was always a great chance to catch up on gossip, find out who was
expecting, who was ill, who was going out with whom, who was
moving away to the city, or emigrating altogether.

Eileen McGrath fell in step with me as I neared St. Joseph's.
Any news you wanted to get around the village, all you needed
to do was tell Eileen and almost every household would know it
before you got to bed that night.

"Well, hello, Delia. Isn't it grand that you can get away to
Devotions? How are things at the Big House?"

She was not subtle, Eileen.

"Ah, I hate to miss my Friday, you know."

"Indeed. Sure we can count on you to be there always, no
matter what's going on. How's himself?"

"Mr. Wolfe is doing as well as can be expected, Eileen."

"Mm. I hear he's pretty bad. Will he get over it, do you think? "

I wasn't certain whether she had actually heard that or if she
was just fishing.

"He's grand at the moment. The drugs are hard on him, you
know. He sticks close to home."

"Ah well, he's always done that now, hasn't he? And his
daughter came all the way from Canada. Then there's that young

one in town looking for her people. By name of Buckley, I hear. Have you met her?"

"Her name is Butler. Yes, she came to the house to talk to me. Sure there's no help I can give her."

Eileen was not deterred.

"But the family she's looking for is Buckley, isn't it?"

"Yes. But it has nothing to do with us, sure. None of us would have known her mother at all."

We walked in silence for a while. St. Joseph's was in sight, so I quickened my step.

"Your sister Maggie, now. She's been away a while, hasn't she?"

"She has."

"Aye. Where is it she is now?"

I was out of patience with Eileen McGrath, but like all gossips she could sniff out reluctance to impart information before a person knew she wanted to keep something to herself and it only made her more determined.

"Still in the home in Dublin where she's been for over twenty years. Doing as well as can be expected."

"Ah, yes. She is. She is. I wonder if she'd know anything about this Butler girl."

"How could she? Sure she was in the home when Iris Butler was born. She'd know nothing. Even if she did, she'd not remember it now anyway. Well, here we are. I wonder what the sermon will be tonight."

"Father Halloran does such a grand job it doesn't really matter, does it? I expect it will be about love your neighbour or some such. You don't have to worry on that score, Delia. Aren't you great the way you look after the sick."

"It's what I'm trained to do, Eileen."

We were at the church door. I dipped my fingers in the Holy Water font and blessed myself. Eileen McGrath and I went in side by side and took our pews.

Instead of listening to Father Halloran's sermon, I thought of the first time I met Daniel. I was working on the children's ward

at the local hospital. Instead of the picnics the FitzGibbons held
on their estate during my childhood, Daniel now came once a year
to visit the children and to read to them. He also gave them each
a copy of one of his books. Although we had lived in the same
village for most of my life, I'd never actually met him before that
I could remember. I'd met his wife and Fran and Jude at those
picnics and run into them in the village now and again when
we were young. Jude doesn't remember me, but I remember her,
always tagging along with Fran, but keeping in her shadow.

In any event, I happened to be on duty the day of Daniel's visit
to the hospital in early spring of 1967. It was a beautiful spring
that year. I remember the scent of lilac as I walked out home after
work and the fields bright with bluebells, all the bushes alive with
sparrows and linnets.

Of course I had seen photos of Daniel. Indeed for weeks before
he came his photo was plastered on every notice board in the
hospital. He was, then, about forty-five, a man at the height of his
vitality. He wasn't exactly handsome, but he had that confidence, a
sense of who he was, that made him seem so.

The children were crazy with excitement. For once none of
them objected to being washed and tidied up. Those who couldn't
get up sat as straight as they could in their beds and those that
were ambulatory congregated in the biggest ward where we had
wheeled those who weren't too ill but who were still confined
to bed. I was alerted to Daniel's arrival by the hush that struck
the ward. It will never leave my mind, that first moment when
I turned and saw him. He stood just inside the door, a smile a
mile wide on his face. I was drawn to him right away, at a glance
dazzled by the energy that radiated from him.

"Good morning, everyone," he said.

Nobody answered, the children being struck dumb by the
presence of the man who wrote the books most of them had
listened to and read just about their whole lives.

"Well, that's not much of a welcome," he said. "Don't you want
to hear about the adventures of Wally Wee?"

"Yes!"

A little girl shouted that out, then buried her head in her book, but emboldened by her, all the other kids joined in. A chorus of yeses rained down around Daniel.

He was wonderful with them. He talked to them very naturally. For their part they adored him. He asked all about them and answered their questions with some humour and patience. He read to them for a long time and I was quite moved to see how engrossed they became, the ward, their loneliness and discomforts forgotten.

My job was to escort him to each ward to see the children who couldn't be moved, many of whom were heavily drugged and often in pain. He was so kind and gentle with them. He read them a story, not too long, and spoke for a moment with each one. As we walked from ward to ward, he asked me about myself. How long had I been a nurse? What did I like about it? When he left I was as enchanted with him as the children were.

The next day he showed up as I was going off duty. He brought a big bunch of lilacs and presented them to me, to thank me, he said, for my work with the children.

"I'm just temporary there," I said. "It's not my specialty at all."

"Doesn't matter to the children why you are there, only that you are."

We walked together to the parking lot. He offered me a lift home, which I refused, not wanting to raise village gossip.

"Can I buy you a drink then one evening? We can drive somewhere else."

I laughed. He knew the small-village gossip mill probably better than I.

"Yes, I would like that," I said, surprised at myself.

I drove into Limerick in my own car and met him there that first night. We had dinner at a lovely hotel. We just talked about this and that, then we drove home separately.

The next week we did it again, but this time Daniel picked me up at the crossroads along the Limerick road from my house.

When he dropped me off there afterwards he kissed me before I got out of the car. It didn't take too long after that before we became lovers.

As I was remembering this I was aware of Eileen beside me, and though I didn't look at her once, I felt her curiosity reach out to me like a tentacle. Not for the first time in my life I was thankful that no one could read another's mind.

13

DANIEL HAD FINALLY AGREED IT WAS TIME TO TAKE UP residence in the room next to the parlour. He had resisted it for weeks, wouldn't even hear mention of it, despite the fact that it now took both Jude and me together to get him up and down the stairs. My day off next day tipped the balance for him. He had to either agree to a relief nurse or move down to the back room. He agreed to move. Perhaps his resistance was because it used to be Ellen's sewing room. At least that was Jude's theory, but when I suggested a different room to him he was no more inclined to shift himself. The room had been transformed into a comfortable place with a bed and easy chairs, a small dresser for Daniel's personal things, and a bedspread, manly colours of wine and deep teal, that was as far from sickroom fare as it was possible to be. I was doing a last check on it, putting a water jug on the beside table and making sure the lamp was bright enough, when Iris's voice drifted in the open window.

"Say what you need to say to him now, Jude, before it's too late."

"It's already too late, I think. What am I going to do? Tell him I love him? That he was a great father? I don't think so. We've come to some peace, talking in the evenings when we were here alone. I think we're okay with each other."

"Don't you love him?"

Jude didn't answer and I almost gave myself away listening in behind the curtain, I leaned so far forward not to miss her reply.

"Well, do you?" Iris asked again.

"I don't quite know. That's as honest as I can be. I have compassion for him now. I do. But love? As a child, I didn't really know him. By the time I was older, I resented him too much. At least your mum took care of you, played with you and talked to you. Even if she wasn't quite straight with you about who she was, who you were, she was there for you. You really had a bond. Daniel and I don't. Anyway, Fran was his favourite."

I moved the sheer curtain aside slightly to better catch a glimpse of the two of them. Iris leaned on her spade and watched as Jude pulled weeds from around a clump of oregano.

"He tries, you know, to connect with you."

Jude gave a small laugh.

"He wants me to take over here when he's gone. Move in and fill it with children. Sometimes I wonder if that's what being nice to me is all about. But I've decided it doesn't matter. Daniel's dying. It isn't hard for either of us to make the effort, really; we don't have to keep it up forever."

She cleared her throat, then tossed aside the small trowel she'd picked up.

"Why do you call him Daniel, not Dad or anything?"

"I started that when I was about thirteen. I was jealous because he spent so much time with his writing. He was either locked into his room writing or away doing school and hospital visits and that. He had no time for us, his own children, so I stopped calling him Father. He had some time for Fran. Likely because she didn't seem to care much whether he gave her attention or not. Besides, calling him Daniel made me feel grown up. Sophisticated."

Iris laughed, then turned serious again.

"Was that hard for you, knowing Fran was the favourite?" she asked.

"Not really. I adored Fran. Daniel and I wouldn't have got on anyway. Guess I wanted a "real" family, like I read about in books. You know, a father who read to his kids, played ball and all that. He did none of it. Even when Fran went missing it took so long to convince him to search for her."

Jude tugged viciously at a vine that had invaded the garden and didn't quite dislodge it. Iris reached for a small gardening fork and began to dig, then dropped it and helped Jude tug at the vine.

"What happened to Fran? I know you don't really know, but I guess I'm asking what led up to her vanishing?"

"Maybe it was Mother's death. Fran and Daniel took that really hard. Fran especially so. She and I were back at university and things seemed to be settling a bit. We were so close. It was my first year away from home and I relied on Fran. I'm still mad at Daniel that he declared her dead. I know it's not reasonable, but there it is."

Iris squatted on the other side of the oregano and began to work on another piece of vine. A crow landed on the fence, its head turning this way and that as it watched them.

"That's awful. What do you think happened to her, an accident or something?" Iris asked.

"I don't know." Jude tugged out a couple of small weeds and tossed them to the side. "She sent me a note saying she was going away for a few days and would see me when she got back. That's the last anyone heard from her. It was only five months after Mother died. Twenty-two years ago. Before you were even born."

Torn between wanting to hear their talk and not wanting to eavesdrop, I hovered by the window. They were quiet then, the only sound the scrape of stones against the spade as it sliced into the dry earth.

"She doesn't look much like you in the photo on the mantelpiece in the drawing room."

"No. She had a head of red hair. It was curly and wild, grew out rather than down. She is, I mean was, older than me. I was always following her around when I was little. Whatever she did, I wanted to do."

The clock on the little table ticked the seconds off while I held my breath and waited for what would come next.

"Must have been awful for you when she disappeared. Do you think she left because she was upset about your mother's death?" Iris asked.

"I don't know. At the time I thought maybe she was tired of the way we both leaned on her, Daniel and I. He completely lost it when Mother died, wanted us near him all the time but we had to go back to university. Fran was like a zombie and I wanted her to be the way she always had been, cheerful and bubbly."

I was lightheaded by the time I let my breath go.

"I wouldn't think that's reason enough to disappear. Or I wouldn't have until my own mother's death rocked me so much. I know I behaved oddly after she died, needed to get away to the hills and be alone, but I would never want to leave my family and friends altogether."

A breeze caught the curtain, which blew in and caressed my cheek. It startled me and I moved away from the window, straightened an imaginary wrinkle from the bedcover, then withdrew from the room.

Time they spent gardening fostered a closeness between them as they dug and weeded and talked. In no time the old kitchen garden was almost cleared of weeds and dead plants and coming alive again with herbs. One more day and the plot would be ready for planting.

Iris had weaselled her way in with Daniel too. Their afternoon poker games after lunch were pretty well established on a daily basis. He hated to lose, and there was much muttering and laughter and thigh slapping as Iris gave as good as she got in the games.

"I have time enough to rest," he said when I suggested he was wearing himself out with Iris. "More than enough time."

There was nothing I could say to that. And though Iris's constant presence irked me I tried not to show it. Whether I liked it or not Iris was now part of the household. I should have been glad that her company cheered Daniel so much, but I felt that one more day of Iris and I would be a total wreck.

Not only was she wearing Daniel out, her presence was also fuelling Jude's preoccupation with her sister's disappearance. One day I had found Jude in the parlour going through photo albums. She had taken out all the pictures of Fran after the age of about sixteen and laid them end-to-end on the coffee table. The earlier ones she'd spread across the floor.

"Delia, come here. Look. Do you think that Fran and Iris look alike?"

I glanced at the pictures. The truth was, there was a very slight resemblance, in the shape of the forehead and curve of the cheek in a certain light, but I wasn't about to admit that, not wanting to fuel Jude's fantasies.

"No more than one person resembles another at any time," I said.

"Really? Do you know, she laughs like Fran. You know the way her laugh starts with a giggle and rolls on into full laughter? Fran did that. It was almost impossible not to laugh with her. Remember I told you I thought I heard Fran's laugh in the village one day? That was Iris."

"Jude, your sister has been gone a long, long time. Don't you think if she were alive she would have contacted the family? Contacted you? You were close, she'd not truly desert you."

"It's so hard to give up on her, though. I think I'm over it, I've let her go, but then... I don't know, it seems impossible. If I only knew what happened to her it would be easier."

She kept her eyes on a photo of Fran. I glanced at it. Fran stood in the arch of Trinity College. The sun was behind her and her hair stood out like a nimbus. She had on a green plaid coat and a silk scarf in red and green shot through with gold.

"You will drive yourself to madness if you keep this up. Losing someone is hard. I know it. But hanging on to the past will just ruin you. Fran wouldn't want that," I told her.

She raised her head from the photo and shrugged, one hand caressing the image she held.

"I know. But I can help Iris find her family. Maybe she will, maybe she won't, but I can help her search. Nobody really helped me search for Fran."

"Didn't your father help? He must have looked for her, surely?"

"Not at first. He kept saying to wait, she'd be back any day. It took him about two weeks to even consider she was missing. She'd left me a note saying she was going away for a day or two, so when she didn't come back within a few days no one worried about it. I knew something was wrong. If she said she would be back in a few days, then that's what she would do."

"The note put him off. It's not that he didn't care, Jude, you must know that."

"Well, if he had spent enough time with us to know us, he'd have known she would come back when she said. Or let us know she'd changed her mind. I keep imagining her off somewhere living her life, wondering what she's doing for a living, where she lives. So I understand Iris's need to find family. I want to help her, you know?"

I did understand, no doubt about that. What I didn't want was Iris rooting around in things that were none of her business. Surely she'd understand that if her mother felt the need to stay away from family all those years there was a good reason for it. Still, I suppose when she died she didn't want her daughter to be alone.

When the end of the day came I was glad to be going out to the farm. A night and a day away from the Wolfe family would do me good. Mam and I were going to Dublin the following morning to visit Maggie. And for the first time ever I was not at all looking forward to the trip. And even less so to returning to take up my duties in the Wolfe household. On the walk home I wondered whether Jude's help would actually result in Iris finding her family. And what else they might uncover in the process.

I SLEPT BADLY THAT NIGHT. THE CONVERSATION WITH JUDE played over and over in my head. At 3:00 am I got up and opened the box I had in the third drawer of my dresser, buried as deeply as possible under what clothes I stored there. Not something I opened often, it held a silk scarf, slightly worn around the edges, a pair of yellow knitted baby bootees, and two folded documents.

The bootees were the one and only things I had ever knit outside of school domestic economy classes. They had satin ribbon threaded through them and were unused, but had grown slightly grubby over the years. Every now and again I took them out to stroke the soft wool, to run the satin ribbon through my fingers. I didn't do it often, and found it especially calming when a child I was caring for died or when I had nights broken badly by strange dreams.

This night I shook out the scarf. I fancied it still held a faint spicy scent of "Opium." The gold thread and colours were still bright, the edge slightly frayed from Maggie worrying at it. I'm not sure why I kept it. Long ago I'd tried to throw it away but couldn't. Perhaps I kept it to remind me of all that I owe to Maggie, or to remind me of all I needed to atone for in this world, but in truth I didn't need much reminding of that. I folded it up and put it back in the box. In the morning I was startled to find that I had slept with the bootees still clasped in my hand. Never before had I not put them away before sleeping.

I lay in bed and watched the shadows from the trees outside sway in the gap of the curtains. Mam moved around in the kitchen, and her sweet low voice carried some old-fashioned tune to me. She loved a day out in Dublin after visiting Maggie. With some effort I heaved myself out of bed and headed for the bathroom.

Dark clouds skimmed over our heads and wind whipped our coattails and headscarves as we walked in to catch the bus, but the rain held off. For once the bus was almost empty and we had choice seats near the front where we could look out the big window. Mam took out her knitting and I put my head back against the headrest and watched as the trees and bushes whipped this way and that on the wind. One of the Reilly sisters sat across the aisle, and soon she and Mam started to chat about this and that. Rain began to batter the bus and my mind skittered around like a squirrel chased by a dog.

14

ST. MARY'S WAS ONE OF THE BEST HOMES IN THE COUNTRY FOR people like Maggie, and was one of the most drear places I've ever visited. The corridor walls were painted in two colours, cream above and green below. Insipid and heavily layered, the paint daubed on with a careless hand, except for the perfectly straight brown line that divided the two colours, doing nothing at all to help cheer the poor souls who shuffled along, feet clumsy from drugs, rarely speaking to their visitors who walked beside them.

Maggie was almost never one of the shufflers, as she was afraid of leaving her room most of the time. She could be chivvied out once in a while, and to give them their due, the nurses tried to get her to exercise, but the poor soul dug in her heels at the sill of the door and wailed long and loudly until she was allowed back into the safety of her room. Her skin had that pale, washed-out look of the incarcerated and her muscles were withered on her bones. Most days she allowed the door to remain open, but sometimes even that was too much for her. She could not bear to look out the window, so her window blinds were almost always drawn and gave the room the murky feel of cave. Mind you, the only view was into a cemetery, so she wasn't missing much. She had been given that room on purpose because she took no pleasure in a window at all.

Our visit started out well. I couldn't be certain whether she recognized us or not. Up to about six months ago she had recognized me most of the time, but now it seemed more hit and miss. I didn't mind too much, as it meant that some of her fears didn't surface at the sight of me, so I was spared her asking about the baby or anything else that she had some vague recollection of from long ago, however mixed-up it was.

Mam fussed with Maggie's hair, which was a rat's nest tangle on the left side where she must have been lying on it. It had grown down almost to her shoulders.

"She needs a haircut," Mam said. "I hate to see her like this. She looks streelish."

She rooted around the drawer of the bedside table, found Maggie's hairbrush and began to untangle the mess.

"Mam," Maggie said, "No." She pulled away and gave Mam a small push with her shoulder. Mam stopped and stared in amazement at her and then looked across at me. The hope in her eyes that maybe Maggie was improving broke my heart. Her hands twitched with the effort to leave the hair alone, to smooth it out, but she knew better than to provoke a tantrum. Maggie sidled up to Mam and stroked her face, tracing her fingers across the lines that radiated out from her eyes, exploring them with a touch that was gentle and curious. She cupped our mother's face between her two hands and gazed into her eyes. They stayed eye to eye for a moment before Mam gently gathered Maggie to her and hugged her. Maggie snuggled into her, sighed and then abruptly nodded off. Mam and I chatted softly while Maggie dozed, all the while Mam's worn hands moving up and down smoothing Maggie's hair, her eyes tear-filled. I left to find a nurse to arrange a haircut for my sister and when I re-entered the room Maggie woke up.

"Did you come to see me?" she asked us.

"We did, pet," Mam answered.

"Are we friends?"

Mam met my eyes again.

"Yes, we are indeed," she said.

Maggie touched the brightly coloured appliqué on my mother's shirt.

"Colours," she said, and began to cry. "I don't like colours. Go away."

Nothing either of us said could console her. In fact, our efforts just upset her more; so much so that we decided it was time to go.

We walked in silence back down the drab corridor and out into a day that was still glowering and threatening rain, heading toward the bustle of Bewley's for tea and food.

⚛

THE SMELL OF ROASTING COFFEE MADE MY MOUTH WATER almost a street away from Bewley's. Inside, we managed to nab a seat close to the fire blazing in the back room.

"That was a good visit," Mam said as we waited for our meal to be served. "At least some of it was. I should be used to how unpredictable she can be, but it catches me out still. I'm not sure they keep her that clean though. Her hair looked like it hadn't been brushed in days."

"It's just Maggie, Mam. She pays no heed to how she looks and you know it. I'm sure she doesn't bother with her hair after they get her washed and up in the morning."

We sat quietly, each sorting out our thoughts and emotions until Mam's tea arrived. Neither one of us ever admitted how relieved we often were when the visit was over. Or how sad.

"God, the tea is only lukewarm. They don't make such a good cup here as Peggy O'Shea makes."

I smiled at her remark. She always had the same complaint but would never let me ask for hotter water, and I had long ago given up trying to get her tea as she liked it.

"Delia, I want to ask you something," Mam said when she'd had a few mouthfuls of tea. "Now, don't be getting mad at me. I just want to ask straight out and get a straight answer. And I want the truth, no matter what it is."

I put my cup back in its saucer, afraid of spilling it over the table.

"You know that girl, Iris Butler, who's looking for her family? She came by the house to talk to your father and myself. Now wait, wait."

She held up her hand when I opened my mouth to speak. Truth to tell, I'm not sure what I could actually have said, because my heart jumped right into my mouth.

"Well," Mam went on, "of course we had no more to tell her than you had, but it got me wondering all the same. About Maggie, you know."

"What does Iris Butler have to do with Maggie?"

"Don't upset yourself, Delia, there's no need."

She laid a hand on my arm. I was upset. I couldn't believe that girl had gone out to bother my mother and father.

"I told her there was no blood connection between her mother and us. There can't be."

"I know you did. She said so. She just wanted to know if we knew any relatives you might not be aware of. That's not my question to you now. I want to know if there is any possible connection between Maggie and her. You know, could she be Maggie's girl?"

"Ah, Mam. No, I assure you. She's not Maggie's girl. How could she be? Wasn't Maggie inside in the home months before Iris was born?"

She looked away into the fire for a moment. Her hand on the table trembled slightly. I reached out for it and held it.

"I'm not lying to you, Mam. I'm telling the truth. Maggie had no child."

"So why does she talk about 'the baby' all the time then? Why does she do that?"

"Because she wanted one. She wanted one very badly. She's just muddled in her head since her breakdown, you know that."

Mam tightened her grip on my hand, then let it go. She turned back to her tea and looked at me over the rim of the cup as she sipped. A log slipped in the fire and sent a shower of sparks up the chimney, blazed and then died down to a red glow.

"You don't think the nuns didn't tell us? God forgive me, but you hear such rumours about them nowadays."

"Mam, I was the one who called the hospital that time when she wouldn't go out to work or eat. I would have noticed. It was only a few months before Iris's birthday. Besides, the hospital would have told us. Stop worrying. Iris is not her child. Rest assured."

"I wish I knew what happened to poor Maggie that drove her out of her mind. She seemed so sensible always. Happy, too. At least after she left the convent. The nuns said she was unstable, you know, but I never saw it then. I thought she was just under a bit of stress when she came out so thin and nervy. But once she got over that, sure, she was great."

She gathered her jacket around her and tucked her hands into her armpits.

"Oh, Mam, we've been over and over this. The doctors say they don't know why she had a breakdown."

"Well, it must be something on your father's side. None of that in my family," she sniffed.

"Mam!"

She laughed and patted my cheek.

"You're a good girl, Delia. Always have been."

The waitress came by and put our meal on the table. Bewley's food was always good but this day it slipped down my throat without taste and lodged like a lump of iron in my stomach. I'd have a word with that Iris Butler when I got back, that was for certain sure.

15

got back. Jude was to go out on a date with Mike. An official date, she told me, glowing with the delight of it. They were on their way in to Limerick for a dinner dance. Jude looked beautiful in a ballerina-length dress of aqua that swirled around her as she walked. Daniel's eyes lit up at the sight of her.

"Beautiful," he said. Jude flushed and looked even prettier. Gone was the pale, tense woman who had arrived on the doorstep just months ago. She had a glow about her and looked younger. She twirled before us and gave a mock curtsey to show herself off.

"You look like a woman in love," Daniel said.

"I think I am in love. I never thought I would be again."

Daniel got up and hugged her, then patted her shoulder so many times she laughed and grabbed his hand.

"Isn't love grand?" I said, but not unkindly. While I had reservations about the class difference between Mike and Jude, I was glad they took pleasure in each other, especially now. It was good to see hope and life blossom among sickness and death. It would be difficult to be unkind to her in her happiness. Before we could say much else the doorbell rang. I stopped Jude going to the door.

"Let me, in case it's Mike," I said. "I'm old-fashioned and think he should wait to see you in your glory."

It wasn't Mike, it was Iris. She joined Daniel and me as we oohed and ahhed over Jude like she was sixteen and on her first date. We heaped it on with trowels, yet the flattery was sincere, and was meant to calm her obvious nerves. About five minutes later Mike came and the two took off in flurry.

"A game of poker then?" Iris asked Daniel.

The two of them settled with a stiff drink and for once I had one myself before I retreated to the kitchen with a bit of mending for Mam. So distracted was I that I poked myself with the needle and drew blood. Somehow I'd have to get Iris out of earshot of Daniel to speak to her. I had got through replacing a couple of buttons on Da's shirt when she came to fetch me. Daniel was exhausted and needed to retire. At my request Iris waited in the parlour while I settled him in for the night. All the while I helped him to bed, readied his medications, and made sure the little brass handbell was in reach, my mind worked out what to say to Iris. I wanted to take her head off, I really did. Yet she was, whether I liked it or not, a member of this household for the moment, a darling of my employer.

As it happened, Iris had something she wanted to say to me, too. No sooner had I sat down than she asked me why I didn't like her.

"I don't dislike you," I said. It was true, I didn't. I disliked that her presence here threatened my peace of mind, that it could bring to light things I would prefer to keep to myself, things I didn't want to think about and was forced to by constant talk of the past her arrival provoked. In some ways that last objection seemed a bit moot, as my whole association with the Wolfes caused me to think about the past far too much, although with them my secrets were still in my control. Iris was a different case altogether. She could delve into the past in a way that wouldn't occur to Daniel or Jude, and there was nothing I could do about it.

"It's that you don't seem to want me to find my family," she said.

"You won't find them at my mother and father's house."

A flush crept up from her throat. She fiddled with one of her hoop earrings, took it out and put it back in.

"I thought they might know some relatives you forgot about, you know. Maybe a branch of the family that moved away from here or something."

"I know my family history. What I told you is the truth, there is no one here related to me who is your family. I don't want you bothering my parents again."

"What difference does it make if what you say is true?" she shot back at me. My hand just about rose to strike her. Shocked, I buried it in the pocket of my skirt and took a few deep breaths.

"The difference it makes is that I don't want my parents bothered. That's the difference."

Iris opened her mouth, then shut it again. We were both silent a moment.

"Look, Delia, I want to get along with you. I won't bother your parents again, they told me exactly what you did. It's not that I didn't believe you, honestly. I just thought they may have, you know, that they might know something you didn't. That's all. As you say, you know your history. You value it. I just want to know mine. Is that so terrible?"

"It's not terrible to want to find your family. No. But it is unsettling to you, and now Jude is reminded of her sister, and it is upsetting her. Your mother kept things from you for a good reason, I'm sure. It's best to leave old things be and not be raking up the past."

I could have said to her that this digging up old bones was unsettling to me too, but I didn't think she'd care too much about that.

"I'm sorry if I upset people. I don't mean to. Jude and I have talked about this and she says it's okay with her. Mum's friend Annie said she thought Mum had been in Wales. I called the hospitals there and a Margaret Burke did work in one of them. They might know where she graduated. Jude thinks we might track down where she came from that way. I'm going over there in a few days to dig around a bit. Someone at the hospital must remember her."

I stood up so quickly the blood rushed from my head to my feet. My impulse was to run out of the room, get away from Iris Butler and the Wolfe family, get away from Mam's questions, get away even from Kiltilly. Maggie was always my go-to person in a crisis and poor Maggie couldn't help me now. Keeping my head and my promise to Daniel to secure the farm could help her, so I took a few deep breaths and offered to make tea for Iris.

⟐

THE DISBELIEF AND ANGER I FELT WHEN DANIEL LEFT ME ALONE and pregnant with nothing but a cheque and the name of an abortionist soon gave way to panic. That we needed to postpone marriage because of his wife's death I understood. I could have dealt with that if he'd stuck by me. Being left alone in my situation was another thing altogether. True, the cheque Daniel sent was substantial. I had no idea how much an abortion would cost but was pretty sure it was not nearly as much as the cheque he'd written. My first impulse was to send it right back. Or tear it up. That didn't happen, because even in my anger and panic I figured I might need that money at some time. Little did I know how necessary it would be, or for what I would use it.

Frightened and distraught, I fled to Dublin and Maggie as soon as we both had a day off.

On the way up to see her I wrestled with the thought of leaving Kiltilly, the farm and my work. I couldn't imagine living anywhere else. Besides, where would I go? Many women all over Ireland found themselves in my position and couldn't bring themselves to admit it or to hide out in the homes for unmarried mothers run by the nuns. Their babies were buried in fields and barns, left at churches. Lucky ones were raised by parents or grandparents, sisters and aunts, who passed them off as their own. During the whole nearly three hours to Dublin my mind ran around and around these options like a cornered animal. Try as I might, I couldn't see past such scenarios. As a result, I fell into Maggie's arms at the station and burst into tears. She hugged me and petted me until I calmed down, then whisked me to a café for tea.

"What will I do?" I wailed as she poured cup after cup of tea that I drank without tasting between snivels and blowing my nose.

"We'll work something out. Don't upset yourself so much. It'll do neither you nor the baby any good."

"I can't get an abortion. You know it. I'll have to go away. Where will I go?"

"Hush, hush. Drink your tea. We'll talk about it when we get home."

I drank enough tea to float a battleship, and by the time we arrived back at her flat I was exhausted but ready to talk sensibly about the future.

"I feel like sending the cheque right back to him, I really do. What good is his money to me now?"

"Don't be foolish. Put your pride in your pocket and take the money. You'll be needing it."

Having already reached that conclusion myself, I couldn't but agree. We went over all the things that were on my mind and came up with no new options. Maggie asked if I'd consider a home for unmarried mothers. Everyone knew how terrible life was for pregnant unmarried women in the discreet homes run by the nuns. I was not about to go to one, nor let them adopt out my child to strangers I knew nothing about.

"Well, you can stay here, I told you that," Maggie said.

"I can't. Mam will visit sooner or later. Oh God, she will be so upset. And what would I do for work? No way would the hospital take me back as an unmarried mother."

"Shhh, Mam'll get over it. She'll love a grandchild when she gets over the shock. Look, I've been thinking. I would love a child myself. My chances are slipping away by the day. I'm over thirty now. Really, I don't even want to get married, but a child, now I'd love that. I could take this one and raise it as mine."

Astonishment and relief made me lightheaded. My child safe, raised by family with no shame to me. I grabbed onto the notion with all my might, even though I knew it was completely impractical.

"You? How could you do that?"

"Well, I could say a friend died and left me guardian. You could see the baby whenever you liked, but I'd be the mother. I'd want it done all legally, mind. I'd be the mother. Legally. It would have to be legal."

Maggie had not stood up very well to the stresses of the convent. I worried if she could juggle work and care of a child, my child.

"How would you manage with work and everything? You know, the convent stress got to you. That is nothing compared to lying to Mam and Da, never mind working and raising a child singlehandedly."

"That was completely different," she said. "I'm different. This is something I want. The nuns were so cold. There was no real caring there. I couldn't stand it. This is completely different. If you could help out a bit financially, I could get someone in to take care of the child. Lots of women do it nowadays. I might even be able to find a crèche. I can show up in Kiltilly clearly not pregnant at just the right time before. Everyone will accept the story."

It was true that since she recovered from her stay at the convent Maggie had been nothing but calm. She had a responsible job. A series of hazy pictures of my child at school, visiting the farm, growing into an adult flashed through my mind. Then I came crashing down to earth.

"What would I do before it's born? I can't just keep on living in Kiltilly, going to work and all that. I'll show in a couple of months. Everyone will know."

Maggie crossed and took a seat next to me. She petted me on the shoulder.

"That's where Daniel's cheque will come in handy," she said. "We'll figure out something. You could stay here; we'd just need a good story for Mam. We can do it."

I knew we couldn't, though. Mam was no fool. Besides, how would I explain just leaving work and going away?

For the rest of my stay Maggie and I talked about her plan for my child. By the time I went back to Kiltilly I was calmer, but still worried about what I would do between now and the birth.

"Don't worry so much, just think of different things you might do. Something will come up, I'm sure of it. I'm so thrilled, Delia. I've always wanted a child, you know that, but not necessarily to get married. It will be wonderful, being involved from the start, then having the baby. For you too, you'll know your child as she or he grows up. Think about that, and you'll find a way."

She was right. The day I went back to work I saw a notice for a five-month training course for nurses in Wales. I could pass myself off as married and work up to late in my pregnancy. I filled in the forms that very day. My application there was accepted. My natural optimism bubbled to the fore as I began to see some way to keep my life in Kiltilly and ensure the safety and care of my child. But within months, everything had changed and the possibility of Maggie raising my child was not a possibility at all.

16

THE RUN OF SUNNY WEATHER HAD FINALLY BROKEN. RAIN
started around noon, a sprinkle at first that blew out across the
inlet, died away and returned about four in the afternoon. This
time it poured straight down, rattled the leaves and thumped off
the earth, spilled out of the eaves, as if it were a waterfall pouring
over the edge of rocks. Daniel and I were alone in the house. Jude
was gone into Limerick to get her hair done. We sat under the
awning at the back door and watched the rain come down.

"It's quiet with Iris gone, isn't it?" he said.

I made some noncommittal noise in reply. It was quiet for me
since she left, but not in the way Daniel's tone suggested. With her
gone I was better able to push down my worry at what she might
find and to regain some of the peace I'd always had in Kiltilly.

"Still, she has to do what she can to find her family, I suppose.
Don't you miss her at all, Delia?"

"I'm too busy to miss her," I said.

"Sometimes I think you're right, no point dragging up the
past, but I've been thinking about it during the past few months.
Natural, I suppose, in the circumstances. I wanted to be a good
man. A good man. I thought I was doing my best for Fran and
Jude when their mother died, but I don't think I was. Nothing
I could do would make up for the loss of their mother. I was
drowning in guilt, you know?"

"Guilt? About what exactly?"

My astonishment at what he said made my tone sharper than
I'd intended. My own guilt had been so heavy over the years I'd

not even considered how Daniel felt. He'd got to properly grieve his wife and hold up his head as a good father and husband.

"About Ellen's death. We'd had a bit of a row before she left the house. I'd told her you were pregnant, that I wanted to do right by you. Afterwards I thought that the row had distracted her so wasn't paying attention to the road."

Once I would have assumed that 'doing right' by me was to marry me. That delusion was long dead.

"She and I talked that night too," I said.

Daniel turned to look at me and half rose from his chair. I concentrated on the way the raindrops hit the ground and bounced back up a couple of inches.

"You did? You never said."

I glanced at him and away. He puffed his cheeks and leaned back in his chair.

"You gave me no chance. It's one of the reasons I wanted to see you so badly right after she died. I wanted to console you and, I suppose, get some reassurance myself."

I'd gone to Maggie then too, as I'd gone to her about my all predicaments. When I confessed my feelings of guilt Maggie had snorted.

"Are you mad, girl?" Maggie had said. "It was the frosty road that killed her, not you. It would have happened whether you two spoke or not. Get that thought out of your head. You've enough to think about."

I repeated her assessment to Daniel, now.

"I suppose so, but how did the two of you meet? I didn't know you knew each other that well."

"We didn't. We'd met briefly at the hospital once. Apart from seeing her around the village now and again, that was it. She knew who I was."

⚛

WALKING HOME FROM WORK THAT NIGHT IN 1967 I'D REACHED
the half-mile mark between the edge of the village and our farm
when I heard a car behind me slow. My heart leapt because at first
I thought it might be Daniel. A Morris Minor pulled up beside
me and Ellen Wolfe rolled down the window.

Even though she was no stranger to me, our paths didn't cross
very often. The two of us looked at each other that day on the
dusky road, me standing almost in the ditch and she in her car, the
yellow indicator extended. She spoke first.

"Delia Buckley, we need to talk."

I didn't say a word. Besides, my mouth had gone dry. A quick
glance up and down the road confirmed that we were totally alone.
I remember covering my stomach with my hands, as if I were
protecting the child I carried from whatever was about to happen.

"Get in, it's cold," she said, gesturing toward the car.

"I'm all right here," I told her and stood my ground.

We stared each down. All I could think of was that here was
Daniel's wife, the woman he had lived with for more than twenty
years. Young and confident of Daniel's love, it never occurred
to me that he may have, probably did, say similar things to this
woman once that he now said to me. Ellen was good-looking. Her
blonde hair swung in an expensive, precise bob just below her ears.
It was too dark to truly read her expression.

"Very well," she said. I thought she would drive away. Instead
she pulled the car off the road onto the verge. She got out. Shorter
than me, she carried herself with a lot more self-assurance, a
woman accustomed to getting her own way. I reminded myself
that Daniel loved me and resolved not to be intimidated by her.

"What do you want?" I asked.

"Daniel told me he's having an affair with you."

I held my voice steady as I answered.

"It's more than an affair."

She looked me up and down, then folded her arms across her
chest as if she were cold, which she probably was in her thin car
coat.

"It's not the first affair he's had, and it won't be the last."

"He wants to marry me."

Angry at how defensive that sounded, I shut my mouth. Ellen looked up at the sky and sighed. The frost crept through the soles of my shoes and I resisted the urge to shuffle my feet.

"He always says that. He can't help himself. He might even believe it for a moment. But that's not going to happen. You must know that. Men like Daniel don't give up their life for girls half their age, who have nothing more to offer than a willing body. As soon as he remembers the reality of the social situation he would find himself in if he did, he forgets them."

It was so calm, this dismissal of me and of the most profound experience I'd ever had. As a pure, simple reflex I slapped her face. "That's what you think," I said. "You think I'm some cheap shop girl who'll crawl away because you say so. But I won't. Daniel will stand by me and his child. You will see that."

Her hand was on her slapped cheek. She removed it slowly. Her face was so white the imprint of my fingers showed clearly even in the dim light.

"Ah, yes, you're having a baby. You thought to trap him in that time-honoured old way?"

"It's not a trap. He knew it might happen. I'm a Catholic, you know."

I could hear a vehicle change gears at the turn beyond my house in the silence that followed. She turned her head and I saw a small sparkle from the pendant that lay on her throat. She laughed, a sneering, sad sound in the dark.

"Catholic indeed."

She turned then and got back in her car. The tires squealed and kicked up gravel as she pulled out onto the road. I remained standing there, waited for the small van I heard to pass, then continued my walk home.

⟁

WHEN I FINISHED MY ACCOUNT DANIEL AND I SAT IN SILENCE for a good long while.

"How terrible for you," he said finally. "Terrible. It was a bad, bad time all around."

He reached out and patted my arm, his fingers shockingly bony against the flesh of my arm. I stifled the retort that rose to my tongue.

"I was lost when she died," he sighed. "Such guilt and remorse. Then Fran disappeared. Jude tried to get me to search almost right away, but I told her over and over that Fran would be back any day. When she didn't come, I tormented myself about that, too. Maybe if I had responded sooner we'd have found her. Over the years I felt so helpless watching Jude grieve and search. I had to declare Fran dead not only for the estate, but to try to put a stop to it. It didn't work, though. She kept right on searching for years."

He let his breath out in a long exhale. This time I patted his hand. The temperature had dropped with the rainfall and I was overtaken by a shiver.

"At least you were all right. I consoled myself with that. I did, Delia. At least I'd taken care of you."

"It's cold now, we should go in," I said and stood up to help him to his feet. We shuffled into the house leaning on each other. It had never been my intention to tell him about the meeting with Ellen. Clearly I needed to guard my tongue better. I might or might not tell him what became of our child that he assumed I had aborted, but other secrets I would keep and take to my own grave. Everything depended on my silence.

17

THE DAY AFTER OUR TALK ABOUT ELLEN, DANIEL DECIDED to throw a dinner party.

"It's time to have a gathering, a really good dinner," he announced. This after he had refused to eat a morsel for breakfast.

"Who'll you ask?" Jude inquired.

"All of us." He indicated the house in general. "And Oliver and Lil."

Oliver Pike was his agent and Lil Rainsford had been his editor for many years. I'd met Oliver a couple of times when Daniel and I were together. In fact, I'd been to a party at his house once, a very tony affair where people drank buckets of alcohol and threw famous names around like confetti.

"When is Iris back?" he asked.

"She's staying a bit longer. There's someone she's to meet who might have known her mother. She'll be back in a few days," Jude said.

"Well, the sooner the better, right, Delia? I don't want to leave it too long or you'll all be partying without me."

He settled on two weeks away, hoping to make it a Friday night if Oliver and Lil could manage it. It was usually my night off, but I wasn't taking much time off at the moment, in part because of Daniel's condition. He needed more care as he got weaker, and although being around Iris irked me, I wasn't that relaxed anywhere else, either, and at least being here meant I had some hope of hearing of any developments. Since she'd gone away, my nerves jangled every time the phone rang. I was beginning to think it would have been easier to tell her what I knew and take the consequences. Times had changed, after all. These days having a child outside marriage wasn't such a big thing. But I had made a promise. Besides, I couldn't imagine what Mam and Da would think about my silence all these years.

"Mike will come, and you'll come, Delia, won't you? You're almost family now, really."

Almost family, indeed. Maggie's face rose in my mind. Not the Maggie I'd seen yesterday, but from when she was fully alive and vital, planning for the baby's arrival reading Dr. Spock's *Baby and Child Care.*

"I'll be here," I said to Daniel.

He and Jude spent the next few hours organizing the dinner. They discussed which caterer to use. Jude insisted that she and Iris would deal with the preparations so there would be no need to get someone to do that. Daniel disagreed. By mid-afternoon they had agreed, at least in principle, on how to proceed. Daniel went to rest and left Jude to call Oliver and Lil.

Over the next few days I saw that the rich don't plan dinners like the rest of us. Their work is consulting with caterers, getting advice on wines for each course, ordering flowers, and hiring people to do things like clean the house before guests come, set the table, and create the general ambiance. It was an eye-opener for me. When we had neighbours in for holiday meals, the house was cleaned, the ingredients were bought, the meal cooked and served all by my mother and myself. Given my druthers, I preferred our way. Still, it was hard not to get caught up in the general excitement. A date was reached. Friday night two weeks away it was. I wondered whether Oliver would recognize me, and if he did, what he would think of my presence in the house.

⚭

JUDE TOOK TO THE DINNER ARRANGEMENTS LIKE ONE BORN TO it. She and Daniel had a spirited discussion on which caterer to hire. Jude wanted to give most of the work to locals and Daniel wanted to use a "proper" catering company from Limerick.

"You know, that's why the locals don't like us much up here in the village. We spend our big money in the city, not here."

"Of course they like us," Daniel said.

"Well, yes, but we're not really villagers, are we? We don't support the businesses here when we could."

Daniel muttered under his breath. Jude was right. The village businesses always needed support, and though we didn't have a catering company as such among the businesses, we had some really great organizers and cooks. Peggy O'Shea certainly knew how to organize and provide good, tasty, first-class dinners and desserts. Whenever the Bishop had a dinner or parish event, it was Peggy who provided the food, and the Bishop certainly liked to set a fine table. The Wolfes didn't understand how scrupulous the villagers were to spread their spending evenly among all the local businesses, shopping here one week, there the next. Most of us went to the city only for things the village didn't provide much of, like trashy fashion clothes, or when we had heavy-duty Christmas shopping to do. When all the clatter of argument died down, Jude and Daniel reached a compromise: wine, decor, and the main dinner from a caterer in Limerick, desserts home-cooked from Peggy's café, and flowers from Mary Ryan.

"She'll do well here," Daniel said to me as I doled out his medications. "I think she'll actually live here as a base at least. As much as I did, anyway. She has a good head on her shoulders."

"Was this an exercise to get her involved?" I asked.

"In part. In part. I really do want to have a nice do here, gather the few people around that I want to be with. I don't have too long left, do I?"

"It's impossible to be sure about these things."

What I said was true, and all this fuss about the dinner had clearly already taken a toll on his energy. This past week, he had stayed in bed the whole day. When he was up and about, his shrunken flesh was hidden by bulky clothes, as he was perpetually cold. Naked, his bones showed clearly through his skin. The excitement of the dinner gave a gleam to his eye, so on balance it was likely doing him good. I took his pulse. When I was done he reached out and caught my wrist.

"Delia, will you help me at the end?"

"I'll be here. I promised you."

He lay back on the pillows and turned toward the window. His chest rose and fell, then paused before rising again in a way I didn't like. He turned back to me and raised himself on the bed.

"I mean, will you not let me suffer? I don't want to lie here, helpless, suffering. You know these." He indicated the drug bottles lined up on the table. "You can fix it for me, can't you?"

He wasn't the first of my patients to ask this of me, so I gave him my standard answer. It's against the law and against my profession and against the Church to do this.

"I can mediate your pain. I will do that," I said.

"Delia, nobody will know you helped me. Please?"

He whispered "please" again. His eyes never left mine as he begged me. I thought of all that had happened between us, his betrayals, the devastation I visited on his family with my silence over matters I could have spoken up about, even Maggie with her tangled mind. All the misery I'd endured and caused lay out before me. No matter what had happened, what was owed or owing between us, I couldn't do this thing, no more than I could have aborted our child. For the first time I realized it wasn't the Church that dictated my actions; it was some innate belief that human life was sacred and was not mine to end. I kissed Daniel on the forehead.

"I'm so sorry, Daniel, but I can't. I just can't."

"Then tell me what to do myself. Show me how much of what I need to take. Some combination of these damn drugs must be able to end it."

The telephone by the bed rang. We let it ring for Jude to pick up. It rang about a dozen times so I answered. It was Iris. She would arrive back the next day.

18

MY OWN SHOUT WOKE ME. I HAD BEEN DREAMING OF something terrible, the particulars of which fled as soon as I woke up, but the hard bang of my heart in my chest took some time to subside. I fancied the dark crawled inside me with every breath, and even switching on the light didn't help. I needed to get outside.

The chill in the night air signalled summer was coming to a close as I paced barefoot hither and yon on flagstones, hardly noticing the cold. It was well past midnight. Sleep was impossible. I would have gone for a walk but for needing to be there in case Daniel wanted help in the night. Jude would never hear him ring from her room upstairs. News of Iris's return, Daniel's plea for help with ending his life, and memories of Wales rubbed me raw inside.

What Daniel asked of me was not an unusual request. Many of my patients asked the same thing of me. They were not really looking to avoid physical pain but the emotional and mental anguish of death, yet most of them didn't know this. They would be in very little physical pain; medication could take of that. I saw it as part of my work to try my best to take care of the rest of it, by being close by, available to take their minds off things when that was called for. I would do the same for Daniel when he needed it. If he needed it. He did, after all, have his daughter there, but often people talked more freely with non-family members, so I would be on hand. No, his request didn't bother me all that much.

What Iris might have discovered in Wales plagued me much more. Names of those I'd worked alongside scrolled through my mind. Would she meet them, would my name come up? They would have no need to mention me at all unless Iris brought it up. Would she? Worry would not change what she found, but worry gnawed at me all the same. The lies I'd told to cover my unmarried state there, and the omissions since chased each other through my mind. If the farm, Maggie's comfort and my professional reputation weren't on the line I would have sneaked off in the dark. Far, far away from the Big House. As it was, I was outside wrapped in a blanket. The wind rose and fell. It troubled the leaves, their rustle growing louder as the breeze approached the house and died away when it passed. It gathered and approached all over again, much like long breaths drawn in and out.

I thought to move inside and try for sleep again. As I turned for the house the wind shifted and carried a faint scent of decay. The rustle of leaves turned into the sound of waves in my mind, and the trapped feeling I'd had all those years ago, a feeling I swore I would never allow again, was back in full force, and my early days in Cardiff were as present to me as the wooden boards I paced on.

THE SEAS WERE ROUGH THAT EVENING ON THE FERRY CROSSING to Holyhead as I went to take up my post in Cardiff in 1968. On the application form I claimed I was married. I had crossed out Miss and Mrs. on the forms, and put Ms., a form of address that was becoming popular. I said that I had kept my own name. Truthfully, I didn't give much thought to the whole women's lib thing, just grabbed onto this because it was convenient. Nobody asked me to prove I was married. I hoped word of my deception and condition would not get back to Kiltilly and my parents. It seemed unlikely they'd hear anything all the way from Cardiff.

The crossing itself was only a couple of hours, and then would come the train ride to the city, which would take about twice as long.

Maggie came to see me off.

"Go on, get on board," she urged me as I dallied on the shore. "You'll be all right. You will. I can go to see you and you can come here, like we planned."

Leaving was hard. I had no desire to live anywhere but where I did. A holiday away somewhere now and again, then home to Ireland suited me just fine. It was Kiltilly I loved. When Daniel and I were first seeing each other he wanted me to get a job in Dublin. I knew from experience that the bustle and noise, the constant traffic, the glitter of shops after dark, the anonymity of the city appealed to me for only a few days. Then pictures of home, the light over the fields, the birds calling from the hedges, the fox I'd see trot across our yard in the early morning, all these things would call me and I'd feel the urge to get back.

"It's not forever," I said to Maggie just before I walked on board. "Is it?"

"No, it's not."

We hugged, then she gave me a little push forward. I turned on the gangway and she waved me on. By the time I got a spot at the railing on deck she was gone. As the ferry pulled away from the dock and the shore receded it seemed that I had my own anchor points to the land that stretched thin and gave me a physical ache. Had it been possible I would have jumped ship and made my way back. Sobs rose in my throat. *It's not forever,* I reminded myself.

As luck would have it, Adele Sweeney was on the ferry. Adele and I had been to secondary school together in Limerick. We'd sat together in our last year because, by the time I got to class that first day, the seat at her desk was the only one available. She had a glint of mischief in her eye back then and it was still there. She was a slight woman, and her natural blond hair was pulled back in a ponytail that reached halfway down her back. Last I'd heard she'd got a good job in a bank in Wexford. Before I could decide how to evade her, she spotted me.

"Delia Buckley," she said. "I didn't expect to see you here."

"No. I didn't expect to see you either."

"Come here, sit with me. We can shorten the journey together."

She patted the seat beside her. I squeezed past the elderly man on the outside.

"You going over for a bit of a holiday?" she asked.

I told her I was going to the hospital to work in the hospice ward. "Yourself?" I said.

"Oh, I've been away to Cardiff for the last few months. I just came back to meet Leigh for the weekend. You remember my sister Leigh?"

I did indeed remember her sister. We had all been at the same secondary school, although Leigh was a couple of years ahead of me.

As it got into the Irish Sea the ferry rolled and pitched on the swell. Adele complained that the rough seas made her queasy.

"Go up on deck," the man nearby told us. "It'll be cold, but the air will help. Keep yez eyes on the horizon if yez can see it. Ye'll be fine."

We took his advice. Night had fallen. We watched the stars duck in and out of the clouds and their light pick up the foam kicked up from the ferry's wake that stretched away into the dark.

"I've turned out as predicted, unmarried and up the duff, nice job in a bank or not." She patted her belly with a sigh. I saw the barely noticeable soft swell of pregnancy. I couldn't think of a word to say.

"I've shocked you," Adele said.

"No, I'm surprised, that's all."

"Not nearly as surprised as I am. I was on the bloody pill, you know. The shite of a doctor didn't tell me I had to be careful for a while. Mind you, now that a baby's on the way, I find I'm quite happy about it. That surprised me too."

A dozen questions whirled around in my head, much too fast to sort them out, never mind ask. Her easy acceptance brought to mind how happy I was about being pregnant when I thought Daniel and

I would marry. Embarrassed, yes, shamed to tell my mother because it would mortify her, but about the child I was happy. I had lost that in my worry since things went wrong.

"What are you going to do?"

The question just slipped out, but Adele didn't seem to mind.

"Oh, I'm going to have it and keep it. That's what I want to do. Leigh arranged for me to stay in Cardiff for a while with a friend of hers. I have a plan."

The sound of drunken singing wafted out when someone opened a door and came out on deck. The man stood along the railing from us and the flash of a lit match flared, followed by the smell of cigarette smoke. Adele watched the tip of his smoke glow and fade.

"God, I could murder a fag, but I gave 'em up. They made me sick as a dog after I got pregnant. Still miss 'em though," Adele said.

We shifted ourselves along the deck away from the smoker.

"Didn't the father stand by you?"

It was a nosey question all right, but somehow the intimacy of the dark and the strange isolation of being on the ferry overcame any polite reticence I had. Besides, she was the first person I'd met in a situation similar to mine.

Adele'd got mixed up with a guy who didn't treat her well. She left him after a few months. He wanted her back.

"He was tormenting me. Called me at work all day long, turned up everywhere. He said he'd always find me no matter where I went. I didn't believe him. I took a transfer to Dublin to try to shake him off. I met a handsome charmer there, Daniel. From out your way, I think. A real gentleman, as it turned out. We had a bit of a fling. Then Jimmy found me again. He'd tracked me down, just like he said he would. He got me evicted because he broke down my door with an axe. Threatened to kill me if he caught me with another man. He would, too, he was that mean."

For a second or two the name didn't register, and as soon as it did my heart gave a terrible lurch. I covered my distress with a claim to needing to get inside out of the cold. By now most people were attempting to grab a nap. A few drunken young fellows tried to raise a song in one corner. Their energy ran out and they quieted down after a ragged few bars.

"So why Cardiff?" I asked when we were settled.

"Leigh found me a safe place to stay outside Dublin. It was temporary and I knew Jimmy would find me again. So she arranged for me to go to Cardiff. She's got a friend there, you remember Margaret Butler? Peg, we called her? She's going to help me. Then I ran into Daniel again, right there on Grafton Street. He bought me lunch and I told him about leaving because of Jimmy, and that I was pregnant. Thank God Daniel is rich as well as a gentleman. He gave me a big cheque to help me out, and the name of some doctor in London if I wanted to get rid of it. I didn't want to, though. I'm using the money to set myself up somewhere safe."

I tried to keep calm while my mind grappled with the idea of two Daniels, two stories of a cheque and a doctor in London. Ellen's words came back to me like a lash: *It's not his first affair and it won't be his last.*

"You won't tell a soul where I am, will you? Promise me." She grabbed my sleeve and pulled on it. Her voice had a rough break of panic.

"Promise me," she said again. "Jimmy McCann really is a bad lot, and I'm terrified he'll find me again. I don't want him to know anything about me or that I'm expecting."

I gave her my solemn promise. She would hide from him; the whole thing was a bit scary, she said, but not as scary as Jimmy McCann.

"I can't tell you about it. I just don't want any way for Jimmy to find out. Bastard. He's made me afraid of my own shadow."

"I promise I won't say a word to anyone."

In part to distract and calm her, in part because I really wanted to know, I said, "Tell me about Daniel."

"Oh, he's older than me. Lives outside Limerick. Out your way. He's a writer, married. Like I said, it was a weekend fling, really, but we stayed friends. He presumed the baby is Jimmy's and indeed it could be, for all I know. It doesn't matter to me; I don't want either of them involved one way or the other. I'm getting out for good. I'm a bit gutted because I won't be going back home again after this trip."

"How far along are you?"

She rummaged in her purse and took out a package of mints. Her fingers worried the foil, grabbing at and missing the tab. I took one when she offered.

"Four months. Well, four and a half, really."

I had to tense every muscle to hide the shaking that came over me. I wanted to scratch Adele's eyes right out of her head. If Daniel were here I'd have gutted him right and proper. Adele asked me again to swear I would tell nobody what she'd told me.

"Jimmy'll never leave me alone if he finds out about the baby. He should never be within a hundred miles of a child. If I tell him it's not his, God knows what he'll do."

Not a word would pass my lips, I promised her.

The ferry was approaching the dock. We busied ourselves with our suitcases. The distraction gave me time to gather my wits at least a bit. Torn between the need to hear more and the need to get away, I went to the washroom. I sat on the toilet and I stifled the urge to throw up.

"It'll be great to have company on the train," Adele said when I rejoined her.

Appalled at the prospect of another four hours or so with Adele, I couldn't come up with a plausible excuse to go my own way. And there were questions, things I wanted to know, now that I was absorbing the shock.

The carriage was hot and stuffy. Adele opened the window but it opened only about an inch and didn't do much to cool us. Finally I had to remove my coat. Adele eyed me up a moment.

"What about yourself?" she asked me, nodding at my belly.

It was a relief to admit it, so I nodded.

"The same as yourself, " I said. "Oh, I was stupid. Just stupid. A married man. You know the old, old story."

She sighed and patted my arm.

"I suppose he's vanished now, back to the arms of his loving wife. We're fools, aren't we? But that's life. You're keeping yours too?"

"Yes."

It wasn't a lie, really, I told myself fiercely. I was really keeping the baby. She didn't press me about the father.

"Well, I have to ask. So does your family know? Does the hospital in Cardiff know you're not married?" she asked.

"No, and no. Maggie knows. That's all. I said I was married and pregnant on my application to the hospital."

She laughed when I told her about how I filled out the forms.

"Tell them he died in a car crash. That'll get you off the hook. Nobody will ask you a lot of questions then. If anyone gets nosey, sniffle into a handkerchief and they'll leave you alone."

We left each other at the station in Cardiff with vague promises to keep in touch. We didn't exchange addresses.

⟐

CARDIFF WAS A GODSEND. THE END-OF-LIFE CARE UNIT WAS growing and the wards were busy. There were endless meetings to discuss how new protocols were going, and endless chats with relatives who came in, nervous and glad of a more open approach to extreme illness and dying. We had a slightly larger staff, because if no relatives were available we took turns ourselves sitting with the dying.

The small flat I managed to get was close enough to the hospital that I could walk there. It was fully furnished and comfortable enough for the months I'd be there. As I settled into the work, my initial panic at my situation died down. I knitted some baby things, including several pairs of bootees. City living didn't really suit me. I missed Kiltilly sorely. Daniel never tried to contact me again. I was now under no other illusion but that the money he gave me was a bribe, a sop to his own conscience. Sometimes on days off I rented a car and went driving out into the lovely Welsh countryside to ease my longing for the open fields and hills around my home.

Too restless to settle into the flat when work was done for the day, I walked the city. The rhythm and the outdoors eased my brooding. I walked aimlessly, sometimes mulling over the events of the day on the ward, sometimes dreaming of my life before Daniel, sometimes of life after my child would be born. I wondered whether the child Adele carried was a half-sister or -brother to my own. In some ways meeting Adele had given me a gift. I didn't long for Daniel anymore. I didn't even think about him much. It wasn't until much later, after all the horrors, that I came to hate him, and feel that he had robbed me of my future.

One evening as I strolled through some of the back streets of Cardiff close to the poorer area of the city, the smell of vinegar from a takeaway fish-and-chip shop caught my nose. The whiff went straight from nose to stomach, and from there it took up residence in the very cells of my body, so that for the next few months I simply could not resist the sharp, greasy odour. On every walk from then on I simply had to have fish and chips drowned in malt vinegar. Sometimes I got them wrapped in newspaper and ate them as I strolled, sometimes I sat on a bench and fed a stray chip now and again to the pigeons. If the weather was foul I stayed in the chippy and ate there.

One evening in early March I was in one such chippy. It was a small place with just three round tables and a few battered chairs. People used the tables to wait for their order rather than to eat, but my feet were tired so I was having a sit-down supper that evening. I had just started my feast when the door opened and in walked Lesley, who worked the ward with me. She was with two other women. Mortified, I realized one of those women was Peg Butler from back home. She had been to school with my sister Maggie. I slunk down in my seat, hoping the three would not notice me. That was a wild hope, because I was the only person there besides the man behind the counter and the cook in the back. Lesley spotted me right away and came over.

"So this is where you hide out. Trust you to find the best chippy in the city."

She introduced me to the other two.

"God, Delia, it's a small world, isn't it? I had no idea you were here," Peg said.

She gave me a wink behind the backs of the other two. The three of them decided to join me at the table. At almost six months it was impossible to hide my condition. Desperate with embarrassment of being caught out by someone from home I mumbled some answer. I gathered by her wink that Adele had said something about me, but she was not about to give anything away to these two.

"How do you two know each other?" Lesley asked.

"We come from the same area," I said. "My sister was in the same class as her sister in secondary school."

"I thought you came from different places altogether."

I wanted to slap Lesley or tell her to shut up, or both. Peg saved me from doing either.

"Oh, Delia and her sister came in to the secondary school in the city. My friend Adele was in Delia's class and her sister was in mine. Right, Delia?"

I nodded agreement. Confidence that she wouldn't say anything to embarrass me grew and I relaxed a bit.

"I'm sorry to hear your husband died," she said next.

I nearly died on the spot myself. A flush rose up so that my face was hot enough to fry an egg on. I looked at her, sure I would find her mocking me, but her eyes met mine, cool as a cucumber. I muttered thanks.

"I didn't know your husband died. I'm so sorry," Lesley said. "You should have said."

"Ah, leave her alone. She's here to get away from all that. Adele is here, too," Peg said to me. "She's staying with me for a while.

You two should get together. She's expecting too. You can exchange notes. She's a bit lonely, I think."

The last thing I wanted to do was exchange notes with anyone about anything at all, let alone Adele Sweeney. However, I was grateful Peg wasn't giving anything away about me. In the end, the three of us walked back a ways together, then went our separate ways home. Peg said she'd get Adele to get in touch, and I prayed she never would.

A FOX BARKED OUT IN THE GROUNDS, A SHORT, ALMOST enquiring sound that startled me out of the past. A lighter blue was creeping over the eastern sky and I was chilled to the bone. Iris would arrive by evening, and whatever she brought with her I would have to face one way or the other. Given her quest, it seemed mean-spirited to have withheld all that I could have told her. To tell it, however, meant giving away secrets I'd sworn to keep and opening the past I'd closed and sealed with as much resentment of Daniel as I could muster.

19

JUDE DROVE IN TO PICK IRIS UP AT THE TRAIN STATION IN Limerick, with strict instructions from Daniel to have Iris say not a word about her trip until everyone was together.

He was not having a good day. He was clearly exhausted, and I asked him several times whether or not he was in pain. He said no. Perhaps he too had had a sleepless night. It was on the tip of my tongue to ask him, but I couldn't bring myself to do it. He made no mention of our conversation of the day before about his death, and I had no desire to talk about it this day. Iris's return stirred up my worries at what she might have discovered in Wales, and I was almost equally divided between wanting to know all about her trip and an urgent desire to be anywhere else on earth except in the company of Iris and the Wolfe family. This resulted in a renewed if unreasonable resentment of Daniel because I had to stay to see that he was taken care of.

"Do you think she's found what she's been looking for?" he asked me at least ten times that afternoon. It was a relief when he went to rest, and God forgive me, I was tempted to give him a sedative, just to keep him from agitating me. I did nothing of the kind, of course, but it rattled me that the thought crossed my mind.

Jude and Iris arrived just after five o'clock. Daniel was up and dressed again, the two of us installed in the parlour. He had been pretending to read the newspaper as he sipped a small Scotch, and I was pretending to read a book, as my brain hopped and jumped around from one thing to another, my ear cocked for the sound of the car engine. As it turned out, I didn't hear the car at all. The two of us, Daniel and I, jumped when Jude's key rattled the lock.

"We're back," she called out.

Daniel tried to get up to meet them, but I insisted he remain seated and went out to the hallway. In truth, I wanted to get some notion of their mood in an attempt to shield myself against whatever was to come, but all I found was the fuss of their arrival.

"I've asked Iris to stay here," Jude said as she heaved Iris's suitcase into the hall. "No point in her paying for that cottage when we have so much room here. I've missed her so much."

I had to close my mouth on the protest that sat on my tongue. It would be well for me to remember this was not my house and I had no say in who came and went or stayed.

"Come in, come in," Daniel called from the parlour.

Finally drinks were distributed and we settled in, ready to hear Iris's adventures.

"Well, how did it go?" Daniel asked.

"Not as I expected," Iris said. "Not at all."

She had met with one of the administrators there, Michael Ledwith, who I'd never heard of, which was a relief, though no surprise after such a long time. He had a file ready when they met, with photos. He showed her one of a group of nurses.

"He pointed to one, and told me that was Sister Margaret Butler. She had left the hospital and gone to Australia in 1968. She came from Limerick."

"Oh, you found information about your mother," Daniel said, beaming.

"No. No. The photo was not my mother at all. It was nothing like her. She was a bigger build than my mother, with very dark and very curly hair. My mum was nothing like that. And she was the only Margaret Butler that worked there during that time."

Michael Ledwith had shown her a second photograph of Margaret Butler. In this one she was on her own, a formal portrait in which she wore her Sister's cap and badge.

"It was definitely not my mother," Iris said, "unless my mother lied about me being her natural daughter. But we looked too much alike for that."

Jude reached out and held Iris's hand. A tear made its way out of Iris's eye and down the side of her nose. She sniffed it away.

"It was so awfully disappointing. Terribly so," she said. "When Michael said Limerick, I was so sure I had found traces of her in Cardiff. Look, I got a copy of those two pictures."

She wiped her eyes with her sleeve and drew a brown envelope out of her bag. She passed the first photograph to Jude, who examined it and passed it on. When it got to me, I looked into the pretty face of Maggie Butler, who had indeed gone to Australia in the winter of 1968. I passed it back to Iris without comment.

"Look here," she said. "I think this is you, Delia, isn't it?"

She handed me the second photograph. Shocked, I took it, but my mind wouldn't take it in. I could see nothing that made sense at all. Gradually I calmed down and was relieved to see that it was a group picture where I was in the back row, my body concealed by two rows of nurses in front of me.

"Yes," I said. "It is. I worked there for a while. It's where I got into palliative care."

"When did you do that? I didn't know," Daniel said.

All three heads were turned in my direction. I looked at each one in turn and took a long sip of my drink. I licked the taste of Scotch off my lips.

"No reason you should, " I said to Daniel. "1968."

Daniel's eyebrows rose, then descended again into a frown.

"Did you know Margaret Butler?" Iris broke the silence that seemed to go on forever.

"Yes, I knew her. She was in my sister's class in secondary school. Then I ran into her again in Cardiff."

Iris's eyes lit with hope. Happy to tell her the truth about this at least, I tried to soften my tone.

"Believe me, Iris, she was not your mother. Not at all. You know that yourself. She went to work in Australia in 1968, just

as that man told you. See, there she is in the front row, quite
unpregnant. This photo was taken about a week before she left.
And I knew no other Margaret Butler at the hospital."

"Oh."

The sound was small and disappointed and it cut me to the
heart. I didn't want the complication of Iris in my life. Not at all.
Still, I felt real pity for her at that moment.

"I don't know what to do," she said. "I don't know where I can
look next, how I can ever find out who my family is. Who I am."

Jude handed her a tissue, then put her arm around her. "We
will be your family, won't we, Daniel?" she said.

"Of course, of course. Look on us as family. You must," he
said.

⚭

"HOW LONG WERE YOU IN CARDIFF?" DANIEL ASKED ME WHEN WE
were alone.

"A few months only."

It is fair to say I wasn't terribly surprised that he asked and I
was glad he had waited until we were alone to broach the matter.

"Hmmf. And you knew this Margaret Butler Iris is talking
about?"

"I did."

"Well? Could she be Iris's mother somehow?"

"Daniel, how could she be? I was at her going-away party
the night she left for Australia. It was the first week of June
and if she was about to give birth, then she's the first woman
in history that did it without gaining an ounce or changing her
waistline. Besides, Iris knows her mother. She told us that. She
didn't recognize this Margaret Butler."

Daniel gave me a sideways glance, then took the pills and
glass of water I offered him. He swallowed them down and put
the glass back on the bedside table.

"No need to be sarcastic. I'm just asking," he said.

"And I'm just telling you. Besides, as I said before, Butler could be her mother's married name. She's looking for a needle in a haystack. Now, is there anything else you need?"

He shook his head no and I could feel his eyes boring into my back as I left the room.

I went to make a cup of tea. Exhaustion dragged at me, and I was looking forward to the quiet and privacy of my room. Iris was alone at the kitchen table writing in her notebook. Perhaps because I was tired to the bone, perhaps because I was feeling contrary, I asked her what I'd wanted to know for weeks.

"So, Iris, you'll be going back to Scotland then?"

"Oh, I promised Jude I'd stay a while. Help out in the garden and keep her company. I think she's lonely as well as sad about Daniel."

"Well, you should be with young people, people your own age. Hanging around us here can't be very cheerful for you."

"What has age got to do with it? Can't you be friends with people of any age? I have fun here with Daniel, too. I love beating him at poker."

I wanted to slap her with a wet rag, but I said nothing. I watched her out of the corner of my eye. Relenting a bit, I told her again I was sorry her trip didn't yield anything useful. She shrugged.

"I so hoped to at least get a lead. It was hard to have nothing at the end. I don't even know now if my mother was ever in Cardiff. There was no birth recorded for Iris Butler there either. She had those nursing certificates, but I don't know if she was a nurse. I don't know what to believe. "

"You know, Iris, your mother probably had a very good reason to do what she did. You must believe that," I said. "Best to let it go now, and get on with your life."

She sighed and tapped her cheek with her fingers.

"I suppose so. Daniel seems so much frailer than when I left and I was only gone a few days. He reminds me of how Mum was at the end. Is he failing fast, Delia?"

"He is, Iris. That's the truth. Nobody knows how long anyone will live but I'd bet he hasn't long at all. This dinner he's so keen on having will definitely be the last social thing of its kind he will have. You can count on that."

"Maybe I'll do what Jude asked me to and stay until he's gone. I want to anyway. I've grown quite fond of him. Besides, what is there for me to go back to?"

I put a cup of tea on the table in front of her. She heaped some sugar into it. The spoon scraped the cup as she stirred and stirred.

"You'll build your life again," I told her. "In time, you'll be fine. And you have your house waiting for you. And you have a new friend in Jude. So that's something, isn't it?"

She nodded, gave a little smile and said, "It is. Yes. It is. She's like the sister I never had, really. I think we'll be friends always."

Nice one, I told myself as I got ready for bed. *That didn't go the way I wanted at all.* I was losing myself in all this mess, one minute wanting to throttle folk, the next feeling sympathy for them. Tomorrow I'd arrange for another nurse to take over so I could have time off. I needed to get away and sort myself out for my own sanity.

20

"AT LEAST IT'S NOT RAINING TODAY," JUDE SAID.

She was driving in to Limerick so I took the opportunity of a lift. A watery sunshine had just broken out after days of low cloud and rain. My spirits lightened with the sky and distance from the Big House. A whole day lay before me with no obligations at all and nothing to remind me of lost sisters, mothers and a dying ex-lover. Jude and I would part company in Limerick and I would make my own way back in time to relieve the nurse for the evening.

"How is your sister doing?"

Jude's question jolted me out of my daydream.

"She's much as always. Mam is going up to see her in a couple of days."

"It must be so hard on you all. Was she always ill?"

How many times had Mam and I considered this as we searched our memories for past signs of strangeness in Maggie? Apart from the time she was turned out of the convent for "instability," there was nothing to put our fingers on. But then who knows how any of us will react to a bad turn in our fortunes?

"No. She was upset by something. So the doctors think. She has withdrawn from the world, that's the best way to describe it."

"It's like you lost a sister too, then, if in a different way. I'm so sorry. I've been trying to accept that Fran is gone, but it's so hard. We were so close. I miss her every day. Every day."

We drove in silence for a while, and I tried to quiet the agitation that was building in me. The road ahead blurred and for a terrible moment I fancied I was driving through the Welsh countryside all those years ago. Jude pulled up at a stop sign and I came back to the present. The car moved across the intersection. Desperate to get Jude off the subject of her sister, I grasped the first topic that came to mind.

"How're you and Mike getting along? Seems to be going well."

Jude beamed. "Oh, it is. He's such a lovely guy. I'm going into the city today to get some art supplies. I'm going to draw him at work. It'll be great to get back to art again. I'm going to set up a studio in the spare back bedroom. I've been clearing it out."

"So you'll be staying a while then," I said.

"Seems so."

We both laughed.

"The house is so awfully gloomy though. I've never felt quite comfortable there, not even when I was a child," she said.

We were on the last stretch of straight road before the outskirts of the city. The morning commuters had gone and the shoppers and trade vans were not yet clogging it up.

"You can change it to suit yourself so you can," I told her. "Completely redo it if you'd like. It's a good solid house with lovely grounds."

"I suppose so. Some nice paint and lighter furniture would help. But it seems a transgression. It's been the same my whole life."

"Well, you've made a start clearing out a studio for yourself."

A small frown was her only response to that. We reached the first of the city traffic and there wasn't much opportunity to say more.

IN THE END, I RETURNED TO KILTILLY EARLY. I'D WINDOW-shopped and enjoyed a nice lunch in the city. I'd sat in the People's Park and watched a small child chase birds and tumble in the grass. The sun was warm, the breeze cool, and together they restored some peace of mind. I picked up a copy of the *Limerick Press* to

read on the bus and a fresh cream sponge cake, Da's favourite, and
decided to go back early to visit with himself and Mam.

The trees were already turning and a light scatter of leaves lay
on the edge of the road. Surprised that signs of the new season
had sneaked up on me, I shuffled my toes through the brown
and yellow leaves, some still soggy from the rains of the past few
days. They didn't yet have the deep musty scent of autumn, and
enough green leaves still hung with the others to form a light
canopy. The sight of our farmhouse cheered me, and I stepped
more lightly on the last quarter mile.

Da was burning rubbish in a tin drum out behind the barn.
He watched the smoke rise and swirl in the breeze before
dissipating. He wore an old jacket that seemed much too big for
him. His thinning hair spiked up in wisps in the heat from the
fire. He turned and saw me.

"Delia, I wasn't expecting you."

"I brought your favourite."

I waved the cake box before him. He leaned over the barrel
and poked the contents with a piece of metal. Sparks flew into
the air.

We walked into the kitchen together. I put the kettle on the
stove and put out plates and mugs while he washed his hands
and dried them on the rough worn towel that Mam kept there
for his hands after hard work. He sat at the table and watched
me go back and forth getting the tea. I put a generous slice of
cake in front of him.

"Are they treating you well up there in the Big House?"

"Of course they are. Jude isn't as good a cook as Mam, mind."

"Aye, her cooking's hard to beat."

"Where is she?"

He took a bite out of his slice, wiped cream from the corners
of his mouth with the back of his hand.

"You look a bit peaky, girl. That's all. Didn't you get her
message?" he said when he'd swallowed a gulp of tea.

"No. What message?"

"It's about Maggie. She's in hospital. Had her appendix out this morning. I drove your mother up but I didn't stay long because of the milking. Maggie's fine."

"Did you see her?" I asked.

"Oh, yes. But she was sedated so I didn't stay longer than to be sure your mother was all right. We booked a hotel for her for the night. She'll phone you later and let you know how things are going. Everything is fine. Don't worry. It'll be all right."

☙

MAGGIE WOULD NOT LIKE BEING IN AN UNFAMILIAR PLACE SO I was glad Mam was with her. Jude's words about losing a sister came to mind as I walked back to the Big House. In those early days I certainly felt I'd lost my sister.

Maggie's decline started with her extreme dislike of going outside. She had a hundred excuses to stay at home.

"Let's just stay in," she'd say when I came to visit.

After the ferry trip I was always restless and wanted to set out on a walk. The need to smell the turf smoke that seemed forever in the air, to walk in Stephen's Green and take in as much of the country as I could before I had to go back to what I thought of as exile, took hold of me as soon as I landed off the ferry. But Maggie would not be persuaded out.

"What are you afraid of?" I'd ask. "You know it's all right. Nobody will bother us."

"You never know," she'd say. "There's always someone around watching. Always. You know what it's like here."

Nothing I said would reassure her. Only talk of the baby calmed her down. She would touch my bump. Each time she felt movement she got as excited as if it was the first time, as if she'd never felt it before.

"Do you think he can hear us? Do you think he knows when it's you and when it's me talking and touching?" she'd ask.

"Who says it's he?"

"Well, he or she. It doesn't matter, I can't call it "it" all the time."

In the end we named the wriggling child "Wogum," which is what I called worms when I was learning to talk. Once, desperate to get out of the house, I asked Maggie to come shopping for baby things. She wouldn't be persuaded.

"You know you'll have to take Wogum for walks, buy groceries, go to medical check-ups once you're a mother," I told her.

She remained unmoved.

"Time enough then. Look, I go to work all week, I just want to stay home and enjoy my place, okay?" she said.

And it was almost okay until the day I got the phone call from her work to say she hadn't been in all week and no-one had been able to reach her. My first impulse was to call Mam and ask her to check up on Maggie, but then I'd have to admit to being in Ireland about once a month and not telling them or calling down to see them. Instead I booked a few days off and got on the ferry once more.

It came back to me, like I was reliving the time I came home to see what was going on with Maggie, the time I realized she was losing her mind, the moment that I could no longer believe she'd come round, return to herself, that I would allow her to be the mother to the baby, the time I had to call an ambulance and commit her to care from where she never truly returned. So many times back then I went over and over it in my mind. In the end I had to consciously banish the whole thing so I wouldn't go mad myself. On my walk back to the village the state I found Maggie in that day came back to me as vividly as when I walked into her flat.

THE ONLY RESULT OF MY REPEATED RAPS ON MAGGIE'S WOODEN door was sore knuckles, so I used my key to get in. For a split second I thought I had made a mistake. I checked the key in my hand as if it had betrayed me and opened the wrong door. The most remarkable thing was the reek of pots left unwashed too long, unemptied garbage, and under it all some rank smell of rotting meat. My stomach heaved, and I stepped back outside for a moment, then opened the door again and went inside. Two wool blankets and a pillow were on the easy chair by the window, and the closed curtains added a murky, nightmarish light to the whole scene. Heart thumping, I called out, "Maggie? Are you there? Maggie? It's me, Delia."

The kitchen clock ticked and outside in the street a bus ground its gears. A small sound, something between a gasp and a sob, made me jump.

"Maggie?"

I took a few steps into the room, stopped and listened. The sound came again from behind the sofa. Maggie was crouched there, knees draw up, peering out from between her hands, which were over her face as if she were a child who believed that if she hid her face no-one could see her. She reeked of sweat.

"What's happened, Maggie?"

"Don't let them in. Shut the door, shut the door."

"It's shut," I said. "Locked up tight. Look."

I pushed the sofa forward so she could see the door. She scrunched further into herself. I eased into her space and sank down beside her. Up close she smelled pretty rank and it was all I could do to touch her, but I put my arm around her shoulders. She leaned into me like a child.

"What's going on?" I asked her again.

"I don't want to get caught."

"By who? Who's going to catch you?"

By now I'd figured out what she was afraid of, but wondered if she knew anymore. Her eyes were wild and haunted, and she muttered under her breath, so I had to ask her again.

"They will. You know who."

I could get no more out of her, so I went to the kitchen to put the kettle on in the firm belief that a good cup of tea would sort some of this mess out. Two dirty pots sat on the stove, one with the lid still on it, the other with a half inch of mould on the bottom. The sink had bits of rotting vegetables lying in a couple of inches of rancid water, scum floating on the surface. The sole of my shoe stuck to the floor and made the sound of a child's sticky kiss when I pulled it free. I backed out of the room. I gave an involuntary scream when I bumped into Maggie, who was standing behind me.

"It's all right," she said. "The door's locked. Nobody's here but me. Nobody. And you. That's all. It's all right."

IT WASN'T ALL RIGHT. IT WAS NEVER ALL RIGHT AGAIN. IN THE end, after I retched a dozen times during the undertaking, I cleaned the flat. I persuaded Maggie into the bath and washed her. When she was dressed and had some dignity restored, I called an ambulance. The next day, after I'd spoken to the doctor assigned to her, I walked through St. Stephen's Green. Up and down the paths I went, hardly realizing what I was doing, until I grasped that Maggie would be ill for some time. All the plans we had for my child would not now come about.

A few days later I left for Cardiff. I cried all the way back, heartbroken for Maggie as I tried to work out how to break the news to Mam and Da. Back in my own flat I locked the door, kicked off my shoes and cursed the day I'd ever heard of Daniel Wolfe.

Shocked to find myself in tears again at these memories, I blew my nose, wiped my eyes and drew the mantle of nurse around me as I walked the last quarter mile to the Big House.

21

"SHE'LL SETTLE IN HERE YET." DANIEL RUBBED HIS HANDS gleefully at the thought. He saw Jude setting up a studio in the house as a certain sign she'd taken to the place. "Maybe she'll marry Mike and the place will come alive again."

There was no point in trying to temper his elation. If she didn't stay, he'd not know about it. Besides, I was beginning to rethink this trait we have to make our wishes and dreams smaller, more manageable. If I had learned anything these last months, it was that keeping hopes and dreams small doesn't prevent disasters. Hadn't I got the means to keep Maggie in St. Mary's just by being bold enough to ask?

"Maybe so," was all I said. "It might indeed be so."

It seemed everyone was settled in except me. Iris had her feet well under the table. She'd moved into the front room upstairs and got work during the busy hours at the café in the village. Sometimes she and Jude worked the garden. Jude had begun to run with Iris on the weekends and they went in to Limerick to the cinema now and again. If Jude was out with Mike, Iris sat in the parlour with a book or scribbled in her journal. To avoid her I took myself off to my room after Daniel was settled. Tidying up one evening I found the *Limerick Press* I'd bought on my trip to the city but never read. With nothing else to do I sat down and read it from front to back. A small column caught my eye about halfway down one page. Mr. James McCann did not show up for a court appearance. He was out on bail awaiting trial on charges for drug dealing and intimidation, and it was believed he had left the country. I wondered if he could possibly be the Jimmy McCann that Adele was running from all those years ago. If he was, he'd improved none in the interval.

⟁

"YOU LOOK GLOOMY," I SAID TO JUDE.

"Ah, I am, a bit."

It seemed like time for a good cup of tea so I put on the kettle while I kept an eye on Jude, who was slumped at the kitchen table, staring at nothing. And it wasn't a nice place, it would seem, by the frown on her and the sighs that wafted through the kitchen and mingled with the scent of almost-baked scones. She'd been out the night before with Mike, and as far as I knew she hadn't come home until almost noon.

"Want to talk?" I asked.

She sighed again, but didn't answer. The kettle came to a boil so I rinsed out the teapot, spooned in loose tea. Steam from the boiling water woke the tannin scent of the tea. I put the pot on the table and covered it with a cozy.

"Delia, do you think it's a problem that Mike works here? I mean, that I'm going out with him and he works here?"

I poured the tea and put the sugar in front of her.

"Well, it could be. Do you think it is?"

"I don't. Or I didn't before last night. It was our first night out with his friends. They were, well, not exactly welcoming. Or some of them, anyway."

"What does that have to do with him working here?"

I was pretty sure I knew, but didn't want to prejudge.

"Oh, I heard one of the guys say something about Mike being on the pig's back. You know, I'd completely forgotten that expression. At first I thought nothing of it, but as they got a bit drunker, one of them said something about his being in with the boss's daughter."

"And what's wrong with that? Aren't you a fine woman? Any man would be happy to be associated with you."

The scones smelled done, so I took them out of the oven and turned them out on a rack to cool. Jude got up and poked them with her finger, then sucked the scorch off it.

"Well, I don't think they meant that exactly. It was an ugly thing, like he was only with me because of who my family is, you know. That we're rich."

"Drunken rubbish. Did you consider at all the difference in your circumstances before?"

It had been a consideration with Daniel at first for me. Yet I let him persuade me it didn't matter at all. My family never had a lot of money, but we had land and enough to keep us happy, so it was not in my mind that money was more valuable than happiness. Not until we were desperate to keep Maggie up in Dublin and the farm in our hands. It never occurred to me back then to consider that most of the money was his wife's.

"No. I didn't think of it at all," Jude said.

I put plates for the scones on the table, then sat down opposite her and fiddled with filling my own cup while I considered how to answer that. I must have been quiet a long while because she broke into my thoughts.

"I never think of myself as rich, because I worked for what I have myself. The only handouts I got from Daniel were my education paid for and a very handsome wedding present. Other than that, I earned what I needed."

"That will change when Daniel's gone. You will need to think of yourself a bit differently, I expect. Mike is a good lad. There's no calculation in him at all. But folks will talk about the two of you. Just ignore it. Eat a scone. They're best hot and slathered with butter."

She brightened and cut into one. The butter melted away in the heat as soon as she spread it.

"At least those goofs' girlfriends tried to shut them up. So not everyone thinks the same as they do. I tried not to let it ruin my night, the first time meeting his friends, but it did. I don't think they're very good friends."

"Eat your scone. Mike has a good head on his shoulders. It'll sort itself out."

I mentally crossed my fingers as I spoke.

"Iris has been in touch with some of the nurses who were at the hospital at the same time as Margaret Butler was there. Don't you think it odd that there are two Margaret Butlers around?" Jude said, licking butter off her fingers.

"It's a common name here. You know that, surely? Half the female population of the country is named Margaret, and there must be half a million Butlers. Besides, she won't learn anything new. I told her as much as anyone knows, I'm sure."

&

WHEN I THOUGHT BACK ON THE CONVERSATION LATER, I REALIZED that between Jude and Mike, my natural concern was for Mike. I'd known him since he was a lad, and he had the most to lose if things didn't work out. He was a good gardener and arborist, but he loved Kiltilly, and work here for him would be hard to find if he ended up needing to leave his job with Daniel. Or I supposed by then it would be his job with Jude. His feeling for her must have been deep to risk that much. Jude would be fine. These days women had so many more options. There was the pill, for one. And other contraception was easy to get, unlike in my day. Not least, she had her own money.

It was clear too that soon I would have to talk to Daniel about our child. At least that. Iris nosing around Cardiff would turn up the fact of my pregnancy sooner or later. Best if he heard it from me. The thought of unburdening it all seemed like such a relief, but in the end it would accomplish nothing much at all. Possibly I'd feel less guilty, but I doubted it. And I couldn't tell him everything anyway, because I was quite sure the whole story would change Daniel's mind about the farm.

22

TRAFFIC IN LIMERICK WAS MENTAL. HORNS TOOTED, ENGINES revved, drivers ran yellow lights, rolled down windows to chat with friends they spotted on the street, and lined up at stop lights like impatient chargers. The new dress had I bought for Daniel's dinner swung from my arm in a glitzy bag. Maybe it was too glam for me. It wasnt like I went to fancy dinners every day of the week. Besides, I wanted to look good meeting Oliver Pike again. The last time I'd seen him had been in Stephen's Green the day after Maggie had moved into St. Mary's. He'd been kind to me then, and I'd needed kindness. A discreet man, he'd never said a word to Daniel, or anyone else, as far as I know, about my being pregnant. The prospect of meeting him awoke in me the young woman discarded by Daniel, and the need to show I had done just fine nagged at me, even though I told myself it was silly. I'd had my hair cut and a touch of colour added at Fancy Cuts in Kiltilly that morning. It had five days to settle before the dinner, and I had a chance to get it fixed again if I decided I didn't like it. On impulse I went into Todd's to have a look at the lipsticks and grab a cup of coffee before heading to the station to catch the bus home.

A woman bumped into me as I dithered in the entrance, torn between a good cuppa or a trawl through lipsticks. We apologized to each other, and I could hardly believe my eyes when she turned out to be Adele's sister, Leigh.

"Delia. Delia Buckley, oh my God, I haven't seen you in years. How are you?" she said before I had a chance to recover from my surprise. To be honest, these past weeks I had thought about looking her up, but had no idea whether she was in Limerick or abroad. She was working in London now, she said, and was just home for a few days to celebrate her mother's birthday. We agreed to catch up over coffee.

"I was just thinking of you the other week," I said after we'd polished off a couple of scones and jam and caught up a bit. "I saw a Jimmy McCann up on charges and wondered if it was the same one Adele was mixed up with years ago."

"Jesus, it is. And they let the little fecker get away. You know, I haven't seen nor heard from Adele since Cardiff. After the arrangements with Maggie posting letters fell through, sure we couldn't stay in touch, really. Then I moved away, but I'd no way to contact her. You know, it was my fault Jimmy found her in Dublin that time. He followed me and I led him right to her. She was terrified it would happen again. You'd think by now he'd have forgotten all about her."

She cut open another scone, slathered it with jam and then pushed her plate aside.

"I'm always wondering how she's getting on, you know? Now Jimmy's afraid to show his face for the moment, she could come back for a visit."

"You never heard from her at all?" I said. "She was very good to me that time."

The waitress came by and cleared away the empty scone plate. Leigh and I dropped into silence. Leigh had a great look of Adele about the mouth, but her eyes were grey and rounder than Adele's. A terrible loneliness rose in me, a sadness for Adele and myself, for the young women we were in Cardiff.

"Do you think Jimmy would still be a danger to her and her child after all these years?" I asked Leigh.

She pulled her plate toward her again but left the end of her scone, then took a sip of tea.

"Yeah, I do. Yeah. He accosted me in the street the last time I was home, asked about her. I told him I'd no idea where she was.

He called me liar, but he went off. He's a right shite, but there's ways to deal with the likes of him these days. I wish I knew where Adele was, to let her know she should come home. We'd be able to get the law on Jimmy these days, not like before, when the police got away with not giving a damn about women being battered."

The information didn't make me feel any better. I don't know exactly what I expected to hear, and having heard this had no more idea of anything than I had before. It was only later as I drove home that it occurred to me I should have asked her for a photo of Adele.

DANIEL WAS DOZING ON THE COUCH, HIS CHIN SUNK ONTO HIS chest. The fire was lit, the first time since summer, and the turf threw off a comforting scent with the heat as I read my way through the *Limerick Press*, something I did every week since I spotted the article about James McCann.

A song drifted from upstairs sung in Iris's beautiful contralto. Daniel stirred, and before opening his eyes called out, "Fran? Is that you?" He struggled to wake. Jude stared at the ceiling with a mighty frown on her face.

"See, I told you Iris's like Fran. She laughs exactly the same way, and her voice is almost identical," she said to Daniel.

"It is very similar, all right. For a second there I was confused."

He yawned once, then the two of them sat staring at the door as the air "I Dreamt I Dwelled in Marble Halls" floated through the room. A door banged upstairs and the sound was cut off. We sat entranced, each one longing for the song to recommence.

"She must be Fran's daughter," Jude said finally.

"She can't be," her father said. "Fran would never have stayed away so long without a word. Never."

"Maybe she was ashamed of being pregnant, or something like that."

Daniel sucked his teeth at Jude.

"Why? Why would she? Her mother might have been upset, but her mother was dead. All we would have done is help her. God, right then new life in the family would have been a blessing."

I stood with such abrupt violence the newspaper fell onto the floor, the pages separating and drifting down into an untidy pool. Daniel looked at me, the light of what he'd just said dawning in his eyes. We stared each other down a moment, then I walked out of the room with as much calm and dignity as I was able to muster.

"Delia, Delia," I heard him call after me, but I kept going. I grabbed my coat from the coat tree in the hall, opened the front door and walked out. Halfway down the drive I had to stop, my legs shook so much. I sank onto the ground by one of the rhododendrons, the damp smell of the earth in my nose.

☯

"DELIA. DELIA, WHAT'S THE MATTER?"

Someone shook my shoulder and called my name. Dazed and disoriented, I came to myself. It took a few seconds to realize that it was Mike shaking me. The sun was low, heralding twilight. Cold to the bone, I shivered and shook like an aspen. Mike pulled me to my feet and put an arm around me.

"What's happened? Come on up to the house. We need to warm you up."

"No. No. Not to the house. I can't go there."

Mike took his jacket off and wrapped it around me. The heat in it from his body went through my thin coat.

"I've got my van. I can take you home," Mike said.

"No. I don't want to go there, either. Would you mind going to your place? I need a bit of time."

He looked up at the house, then back at me. I put a hand on his chest.

"Please."

"Yeah, okay."

He shrugged and held my arm as we went through the trees to where he kept his van. We rattled our way out to the small cottage on the road to Knockdeara.

"You all right to make your way in?"

"Yes. I'm fine. Really. I just need time to...just time."

Mike stood aside to let me in the door ahead of him. Warmth from the big range that dominated the room wrapped around me. It was a good-sized room with a big window that overlooked a garden. Bird feeders hung on the clothesline, and sparrows, finches and tits flitted back and forth and clung to the feeders, filling up before night fell. I couldn't take my eyes off them. From behind me came the squeak of a tap turned and the sound of water hitting the metal of a kettle.

"We think it cures everything, don't we?" I said.

"What? Oh, the tea. Yeah, we do. Sure it's been keeping our heads above water for generations."

We didn't say much until we'd had our first cup. As Mike poured the next he asked me if I wanted to talk about whatever it was.

"I do, and I don't. It is something that shouldn't matter now, that took me by surprise. I think I'm being oversensitive, is all."

I was being no such thing. Daniel's words had hit me right in the heart. Clearly our child and I had meant little or nothing to him or he would never have said that. Whatever idea I had to tell him about the birth was gone, and I wondered whether my urge to tell him was an attempt to shame him. Or maybe to pass off some of my own guilt.

"Well, you seemed pretty upset. Anytime you want to talk, I'm here."

I almost told him then. Most of it, anyway. Until I remembered he and Jude were in love and he would naturally want to share whatever I said. He certainly didn't deserve the burden of keeping my secrets, so I thanked him and held out my cup for a refill.

THE LIGHT WAS ON OVER THE FRONT DOOR OF THE BIG HOUSE. AT the bottom of the step my feet stopped of their own volition and I had to make a real effort to walk up and open the door. As soon as I was inside, Jude came out of the kitchen, took a few steps forward, then stopped. My own steps faltered. The hallway stretched between us, filled with the cloying scent of the lilies in their vase on the table.

"Hello," I said finally.

Embarrassed by my earlier flight from the place, and with no real idea of what to do now, I shut my mouth. Had I not had my professional persona to worry about, I wouldn't have come back at all. As it was, I was weighing the cost of quitting against that of staying. In my heart I knew I would stay for the sake of the farm. I didn't like that feeling at all. The only consolation was that my time at the Big House would soon be over.

"Delia, I'm glad you're back. I've got Daniel into bed for the night. Sort of, anyway. Come on and have some tea."

Jude came forward and helped me off with my coat. Tea was the last thing I wanted, as I was ready to float away, I'd had so much at Mike's.

"Thanks. I don't need tea. Sorry I wasn't here to help Daniel."

The disembodied feeling I'd had by the rhododendron bush was back. Was this what had happened to Maggie, she just disconnected and couldn't get back?

"On second thoughts, tea sounds good," I said.

Jude ushered me into the kitchen. I sat in Daniel's usual chair, then got up and went to the other end of the table. I'd turned down Mike's offer of a lift and walked back. I was once again cold to the bone from the evening air.

"I put your dinner in the oven, if you're hungry," Jude said as she put a mug of tea in front of me.

"Maybe later. Look, I'm sorry I rushed off. I...I read something in the paper that gave me a shock."

It was the best explanation I could come up with, certain that Daniel hadn't told her why I might be upset. He hadn't, apparently.

"Oh, poor you. Do you want to talk about it?"

"No, no need. It was foolish of me to run off."

We sat together and sipped our respective teas. I wanted to say something to her about Iris but couldn't come up with the right thing. Aware that Jude was studying me when she thought I wasn't looking, I tried to keep my face neutral.

"Delia, there's something I want to talk to you about. Look, I'm not trying to be nosey here, but one of the people Iris talked to in Cardiff said that you were married. You never mentioned it, and no reason why you should, but she also said you had a baby. I... well, I'm curious, that's all."

I put my cup down carefully on the table, glad that most of my emotional coin had been spent earlier, such that I had no energy left to react with either much alarm or surprise.

"It didn't seem relevant. Is it?"

"No, no. I don't suppose so. It's just that I know your husband died, and I was wondering about your child."

"Is this because of Iris?" I asked.

A flush rose up her neck to her forehead. She dropped her eyes, shrugged one shoulder, then very quietly said, "Yes."

It was my turn to sigh. The clock chimed the half-hour and one of the kitchen cupboards settled with a creak.

"Jude, I have told all I can about Iris. There's nothing more to say on that score. My private life doesn't need to come into it."

Jude nodded.

"Well, to be honest, I don't think Iris has anything to do with your private life. I think she's probably Fran's child."

"Do you really think your sister would have said not a word to you all these years if she were able to?"

As I spoke the words I realized that this was exactly what Adele did with her family. That Adele and Leigh were close was certain, yet because of the danger Adele was in, she cut off all connection with her family.

"I believe she would have. I want to believe she would have. But the similarities are uncanny between Iris and Fran. Uncanny. The more I get to know her the more I see it."

Her eyes were pleading. I tried desperately to find some way out of my dilemma.

"You're seeing what you want to see. Well, there is one way to be sure. You could try one of those paternity tests, but they're expensive. They're not perfect but could tell you if she is related to you."

"Do they do it here, in Ireland?"

"I'm not certain. You could find out easily enough, I should think. Mind you, Iris will have to agree."

Jude got up and paced the length of the kitchen table, then turned abruptly and made her way back.

"I haven't said anything to Iris about who I think her mother might be. You know, I didn't think of a test."

She stopped and leaned across the table to me. Her eyes tried to crawl inside my skull to find what I thought.

"Well, just don't raise her hopes too high. Or your own, either," I said. "I very much doubt she's Fran's child."

"I'll think about it. Thank you. Thank you for suggesting the test. It would ease my mind to know."

"And if she isn't? What then?"

"Then I'd know. At least that."

I stood up myself, bone weary and longing for my own room and my own company.

"Yes, you would. But if she's not related to you it wouldn't do much for Iris, though, would it?"

23

"I'M SORRY, DELIA. FOR WHAT I SAID EARLIER ABOUT NEW LIFE in the family. I'm a fool," Daniel said.

It had taken all my discipline and self-control to go into the room and check on him before I went to bed. Outside the door I had to pause to set my face in neutral and to still the tremble in my hands. He lay on his pillows, tense as a board, his eyes glued to the doorway when I finally went in. Before I could get a word out he blurted out his words of apology. I had no answer to them.

"Are you all right for now?" I asked.

"Delia, really, I'm sorry. I spoke without thinking. Can we talk about it?"

"About what?"

"What I said that made you run off like a scalded cat."

His room was perfectly tidy, but I made a display of straightening his shoes by the bed and resettled his clothes on the back of the chair. There was not a word I could think of to say on the matter. Torn between the desire to take his head off, to tell him exactly what I thought of him, and the desire to walk away out of the house, never to come back, I said, "Are you settled now? Do you need anything?"

"Ah, Delia, please. I am sorry. I really am."

My arms folded themselves across my chest. I uncrossed them and let them hang by my sides. "Daniel, I'm unsettled by all this harping on about the past that goes on in this house, that's all. What does it matter in the end? Fran is gone; Iris's mother is dead. Nothing is going to change that. The likelihood of Iris being Fran's daughter is remote at best. Let these things go. Stop all this bloody talk about it."

His eyes were on me all through this tirade. When I was done he reached out to touch me. I took a few steps back.

"It's not so easy to let it rest. Jude could be right; Iris could maybe be her niece, my grandchild. That's not what I am saying sorry about. You know that. It's not what sent you running from the room."

"No. It isn't. 'Twas hearing you say that our child, my child, was nothing to you. It was a shock to hear the words from your very mouth, even though it was not news to me. I knew it the day you mailed me that cheque. What you said, that simply confirms it in no uncertain terms. All that too is in the past. I've nothing to say about it. Now, if there's nothing else you need for the moment, I'm off to bed."

That night I decided never to say a thing to Daniel about our child. Not even if Iris and Jude came up with proof positive that I was pregnant. Adele's indifference to who her child's father was came back to me and I finally, thoroughly understood it.

ADELE HAD HER FEET UP ON AN OTTOMAN IN MY LIVING ROOM in Cardiff. Try as I might not to think about how weird it was that we had become friends, every now and again it got to me. Yet friends we were. Truthfully, it was a relief to have her to talk to. No pretense was necessary with her, and to a fair extent she understood everything I was going through, as she was pretty much in the same boat. The one big difference between us was under discussion this particular day.

"Which one of them is the father doesn't bother me all. It will make no difference to how I feel about the child," she said. She munched on a custard cream biscuit and a small scattering of crumbs sprayed out as she spoke.

"What if it's Jimmy's? Won't it drive you crazy to know he's the father?"

"Not at all. It's not the child's fault. Will you resent yours because of the father?"

Of course my answer was no. But I wasn't as indifferent as she was to the matter of the father. Perhaps in asking her all these questions in my own way I was trying to think how much Maggie and I would tell this child later. Although I supposed Maggie would have the main say in that, at least while the child was a minor. While I took Adele's point that it wasn't the child's fault, and it wasn't, there seemed to me to be a difference between telling a child who its father was and not knowing.

"Well, anyway, I want my child to have nothing, absolutely nothing to do with that Jimmy McCann. Not ever. Promise me, Delia, you will say nothing about my child to anyone."

It was a promise she extracted from me on a regular basis. I agreed, as usual.

"If anything happens to me, will you look out for my baby? Make sure she never has anything to do with him? Will you?"

That too was a familiar promise. And I promised. We agreed that somehow she would send word to me if anything happened to her.

"Nothing will happen to you."

I said this regularly, too, and I even believed it. I understood her need to keep her child safe from this Jimmy. Somewhere in the middle of all these discussions I managed to persuade myself that the child she carried was not Daniel's.

"What will you tell him later, or her? Later, what will you say when they ask?"

"I'll worry about that then. For sure I'll say nothing until I know we're safe from Jimmy. So I suppose I'll say I've no relatives, which in its own way will be true, won't it?"

In that moment I felt completely lucky that I had Maggie to step in. The child would be surrounded by true blood relatives.

"Hey, you still won't tell me who the father of yours is?" Adele asked.

"What possible use could that serve? He's not involved, and maybe we'll tell later, when the child is all grown up, or maybe we won't. Right now, I don't care about all that."

Adele was entering her eighth month and I was just over seven. My exile was weighing on me, and so were the stories I had to maintain, both the one in Cardiff and the different one for my mother and father across the sea. Time had begun to drag, and without Adele, with whom I could simply be myself, I don't know how I would have managed. The following week I was going to visit Maggie, and with every passing day I grew more and more impatient to see her, to make sure everything was ready for the baby, to catch the scent of turf in my nose and readjust my ear to the rapid-fire gab and lilt of home accents.

"Do you want me to take a letter for you to Leigh?" I asked Adele.

Whenever Maggie visited or I went to Ireland, we took a letter to post there to Leigh from Adele, whose paranoia about Jimmy was so profound that she wouldn't even send a letter from where she lived. Leigh's letters went to Maggie, and Adele's went to Maggie, who posted them on. They were carried back and forth across the sea by whichever one of us was making the trip. It was her only contact with family. Adele figured she could keep on with this after she went into hiding, get a post office box somewhere and use Maggie to post the letter from Ireland. We had it all worked out, even though Adele would still not tell me the full extent of her plan, or where she intended to live.

So I took the letter that time, but it wasn't posted until much later. Things happened. Terrible things that changed everything for Maggie, Adele and me.

24

THE NEXT DAY, PLANS FOR THE DINNER ON FRIDAY WERE IN FULL swing. Mike had to be dragooned into dealing with the dining room table, which hadn't been used for so many years the runners were too stiff to be moved without serious manhandling and oiling.

"It's a fine room, isn't it?" he said to me when the table, two leaves inserted, was sitting in the middle of the room waiting to be polished.

"'Tis. Pity it's not used much. Look at the light, and the views."

The dining room had windows on two sides, one facing west out over the meadow and the other facing south, framing the tree-lined path that led deep into the estate.

"I guess this will all be Jude's when her father goes. Funny, I hadn't really given it much thought until recently."

"'Til your friends remarked on it, is it?" I said. I gave him a smile to show I meant no harm by the question.

"Oh, you heard, so? I suppose I'm reaching above myself a bit, but I truly care about her, Delia, not her money."

I patted him on the shoulder.

"Well then, don't be listening to drunken rubbish. Show her you care for her, that's the best you can do. Daniel Wolfe had barely two ha'pennies to rub together when he married Ellen."

A quick dip of his head to one shoulder was his only answer. We surveyed the room again. Mike ran his hand over the smooth finish of the teak.

"It'll be lovely when it's oiled, so it will. A thing like this needs care."

We stood in contemplation of the table for a few minutes before he asked me how I was doing.

"You know, after the other day?"

"Sure I'm fine, Mike. I am. Just had a bit of a shock, you know. But I'm all right now."

Before either of us could say more Jude arrived with the teak oil.

I WAS FAR FROM ALL RIGHT. MY NERVES WERE IN BITS THINKING about the dinner coming up. Of course I could always not go, but what explanation would I give? And what was I to do, hide in my room? Take the night off and get in a relief nurse? Any more talk of Fran or Iris's parentage and I'd go right round the bend. It was a relief to go meet Mam at Peggy O'Shea's for an hour in the afternoon. She'd been up to see Maggie again and I met her off the bus.

"She's fine since she's back in St. Mary's. Still a bit sore after the appendix, I think, but no worse than usual in herself."

I was glad to hear it. Since Maggie'd been sick, something of the nightmare quality of the time of her breakdown had been invading me, along with worry for her.

"You don't look like yourself, Delia. Is everything all right?"

My first impulse was to snap at her. If people didn't stop asking me if I was all right I was bound to snap at someone. I took hold of myself and managed to answer mildly enough, "I'm fine, Mam. Fine. How's Da?"

Mam wouldn't be put off. "I'm not sure working up there is good for you." She gestured with her thumb in the general direction of Daniel's place. "It's great that the mortgage got settled and I'm grateful to him for that, but not if it means you running yourself down."

"I'm not running myself down, Mam. Sure I've less to do there than most places. Jude is there and now Iris is there too."

"Iris? She's moved in there? It's nice of them to take her in, isn't it?"

I could have kicked myself for mentioning it. The last thing I wanted was to bring all that up again.

"Yes. She and Jude are great friends. She's no bother to me and she keeps Daniel amused."

Peggy arrived with our scones and by the time we'd exchanged pleasantries with her and Mam had praised her baking, I'd thought of other things to talk about. Mam wasn't about to let things go, though.

"Look, have another scone, put back some of that weight you've lost. It doesn't do to get thin at your age, you know. You'll end up looking scrawny."

I had to laugh. The last time my mother had called me scrawny was when I went home after the baby was born. I was scrawny then. I'd lost so much weight I'd had to buy new clothes to wear and not only because I no longer needed maternity things.

Mrs. Cleary stopped by our table and of course Mam asked her to join us. Soon the two of them were into discussing Mary Robinson's chance of being elected president in the upcoming election.

"It'll change things for the women of Ireland, having a female president," my mother declared. "We'll be second-class citizens no more, I tell you."

"I should think so. The women will all come out and vote for her. She'll be a shoo-in. Sure, even America never had a woman president."

"Oh, yes. We'll finally get a say in things. And we can thumb our noses at those who think we're a backward country. Look at all the changes in the last ten years."

Mam waved her butter knife around like she was about to slay a dragon. She was so much more at ease since the farm was re-mortgaged and the worries about money had abated, which put me in mind of Daniel and his money.

&

AFTER A FEW WEEKS IN THE PSYCHIATRIC WARD MAGGIE SHOWED no real improvement. I was worn out from working and then going back to Dublin for one or two nights on my time off, then back to work again. The hospital suggested I find a nursing home for her, so I checked out St. Mary's, which was considered to be the best facility of its kind in the land. My next challenge was telling our parents. The proper thing would have been to go down to tell them in person. I ruled that out, given my condition and their ignorance of it. Because we didn't have a phone in at the farm yet, I made arrangements with John Joe up the road that Mam would be there to take my call.

"What is it? Are you all right?"

As usual she shouted into my ear, cutting to the chase as she talked over my hello. I broke it to her as gently as I could. She was incredulous.

"But Maggie's never had problems like that. Never."

"Well, there was that time she was sent home from the convent."

"Ah, that! That was only strain because the life didn't suit her. It's not the same. Something must have happened."

"Well, a shock of some kind, the doctor says. Sometimes a breakdown just happens."

Apart from some small, inconsequential social lies, I'd never lied until Daniel and I began to date. Since then I'd done nothing else, it seemed to me. Lies were like a fungus, spores grew out of each other until the original thing was covered and distorted by the overgrowth, totally unrecognizable as itself. The lies I had to tell made it harder to counter my own shock at this turn of events. There would be no question now of Maggie taking my child, and I had no idea in the world what I would do.

25

THE RECENT EASE BETWEEN DANIEL AND ME HAD NOT returned by the day before his dinner. Fresh flowers were in almost every room, bedrooms had been aired out, all the preparation and the cleaning done by Marg Hislop and her daughter. The caterers would arrive next day. In Daniel's case, rest would have been a good thing, but he was too keyed up. Jude worried he'd wear himself out and not be able to sit at the dinner table.

"Don't worry about me," he told her. "I'll be there no matter if the sky falls. I've been looking forward to this ever since I thought of it."

But in fact there was nothing to do but wait until his guests arrived next day, and he finally agreed to lie down for a while in mid-afternoon. Exhausted as well as nervous about seeing Oliver Pike again, I sat in the parlour and tried to read a book. Jude was there polishing the silverware that was already gleaming. I fretted that Oliver might let on Daniel and I knew each before, but I consoled myself that as a literary agent to the like of Daniel and other such men, he must be able to keep a discreet tongue in his head.

"Delia, has something happened between you and Daniel?"

Jude's voice made me jump. Unwilling to talk about it, I tried to marshal my thoughts.

"I mean, it seems a bit distant between you this past week. It's none of my business, I know, but if I can do anything to smooth things over, or if you want to talk, I'm here."

I fairly trembled with relief. Surprised and a bit touched that she cared and offered, I had to stop my eyes from filling. I gave myself a good mental shake and tried to get a grip. Not a person who cried easily, I'd been on the verge of it way too often these past couple of weeks.

"It's nothing to worry about, Jude. Daniel is preoccupied with this dinner, and I've been chivvying him to take it easy. You know he hates that."

As an explanation it would do. In any case, it was the best I could come up with.

"I've thought about what you said about Iris and a paternity test. Daniel would have to agree. I'll ask Iris to do the test after this is over. If she doesn't want to, or is hesitant at all, I'll let it go."

"Good. Good. I'm sure she'll agree. But make sure she's comfortable with it if it turns out to be a disappointment. You know how upset she was when nothing came about in Wales."

Some of my tension left with this news. It would take some of the weight off my shoulders about Iris, bring us one step closer to resolution, without me having to say anything at all. Even so, I worried that if the test turned out negative, Iris would be despondent. It would close another door, one she must herself be thinking about. In this I was wrong.

No sooner had Jude finished her polishing and gone back to the dining room than I took myself off for a walk. At the cross between the road into the village and the one out of it, it struck me that I had nowhere to go. Our farm offered no comfort to me this day, and my stomach had no place for a piece of Peggy O'Shea's pie or her questions. In the end I turned to the road out towards Knockdeara. When I reached the hill topped by the oak I climbed over the low wall and made for the tree I had come to think of as my tree. Spread out below me was the village on one side, the pier and harbour on the other, and behind the drop to the road to Knockdeara.

It was just about suppertime and the parade of cars back into the village was underway, the whine of their engines as they tackled the hill a counterpoint to the cawing of crows. Four magpies foraged down the slope from me. *One for sorrow, two for joy, three for a wedding and four for a boy.* The old rhyme came to me as I watched them. The crows croaked protest at the invasion of their territory. The magpies took no notice. From the hill the change in colour of the trees created a fine muted patchwork of brown and gold against the turned earth of the farmers' fields. A few Holsteins lying under the trees a few fields away complained they needed milking. I took a deep breath and settled my back against the oak. Gradually the smaller sounds penetrated, the distant low of a cow, an unarticulated shout from one of the sailors on the pier, the flap of a crow's wing as it lifted over the treetop.

My mother and Mrs. Cleary had it right. Things had changed since 1968. I was, after all, a grown woman. Whatever came out about me now would be old news, a nine days' wonder, and life would go on. The onslaught of memories assailing me from being around Daniel, June and Iris had exhausted me. Since I had lost myself under the rhododendron in the driveway, terror that I would go the same way as Maggie haunted me and drove me to a decision. I was finished with hiding things and lying. Iris was grown up and could make her own decisions. I would have to talk to Mam. Soon. There under the oak, I made a solemn promise to myself and Maggie that, no matter what, I would never speak to another living soul about the thing that ruined her. That part of the story I would keep to myself. I rose as the sky dimmed, and with more peace than I'd had since Daniel Wolfe approached me in Peggy O'Shea's café, I headed back to the Big House. The first thing on my list was to put a call through to Leigh Sweeney.

26

FOR THE FIRST TIME IN WEEKS I SLEPT LIKE ONE DRUGGED: soundly and late. I threw back the curtains to a lovely autumn day. The sky was a cloud-studded blue that faded out toward the horizon. Jude was raking leaves from the driveway amidst a shower of brown, yellow and red that littered it again as soon as she cleared it. The pines looked dark and stoic amid the autumnal glory. Being late, I turned away from the window and dressed in a hurry, then made my way down to check in on Daniel.

"Well, Delia, " he said when I went in. "Today's the day."

"It is indeed, Daniel."

As I got him ready for his big day, helped him wash, as my fingers rippled across the washboard that was his backbone, I remembered him as he was when I loved him. Handsome. Solid. He had the determination and charm that a young, naive woman like I was then took for something I could have by proxy.

"Do you remember Adele Sweeney?" I asked him.

"Adele? Sweeney? No, I can't say I do. Should I?"

The soap slid down his back chased by water from the showerhead. I thought of the baptism of my child, the water that ran over his forehead and startled him, so that his hands spread like starfish and his eyes opened blue and wide.

"Doesn't matter," I said.

☙

WHEN OLIVER AND LIL DID ARRIVE, I WAS IN MY ROOM. DRESSED for dinner, I twisted and turned to examine my reflection in the wardrobe mirror for any little imperfection. The doorbell chimed and Oliver's voice rumbled up to me as Jude greeted him at the door. I gave my shoulders a last brush-off and emerged on the landing at the same time as Iris. She wore a dress that matched exactly her cornflower-blue eyes and fell in soft folds to just above her knees. Her usual boots were replaced by high heels. She wobbled slightly as we walked towards the stairs.

"High heels kill me," she said.

"Well, you don't have to go far."

She smiled at me and I saw her mother in her. I touched her cheek.

"You look beautiful," I said.

She beamed. I wanted to stand there forever, exactly so, both of us in our finery, to keep the warmth between us. Perhaps this one evening could be calm, social between us all, with no questions about the past. Perhaps I could simply enjoy myself in the moment and put off all the unravelling of the past that would leave in its wake who knew what? I kissed her on the cheek and took her arm in mine. She gave me a glance of surprise and, maybe, a little apprehension, before she laughed and we descended the stairs together.

27

DANIEL HAD JOINED JUDE, LIL AND OLIVER IN THE FOYER.
Oliver had lost some hair, found a small paunch, grey hairs and
few lines, but was otherwise unchanged from when I last saw
him.

"Delia," he said, "what a surprise. I'm so glad you and Daniel
made up. Is this your daughter?"

Iris's arm disengaged from mine as I heard her gasp.

"Hello, Oliver. No, she's not my daughter. And I'm Daniel's
nurse." I put an emphasis on nurse.

Oliver flapped his hands, looked behind him for rescue which
wasn't there, and smiled so much I thought his face might break.

Daniel introduced Lil. She was close to six feet tall. Statuesque.
Her hair was long and dark brown mixed with grey. It hung
right down to her waist. She wore flat shoes and no makeup.
She exuded the energy you imagined Boudicca leading the Iceni
might possess. I felt completely overdressed next to her.

"Oh, sorry, who is this lovely person?" Lil asked.

I introduced them, and we all made our way into the parlour.

&

After general chat and drinks in the parlour we were finally
summoned to the dining room by Jude. The room was transformed.
The big teak table was covered by a beautiful damask cloth on
which the place settings and glasses gleamed. Small rose posies
dotted the length of the table together with silver candleholders

with tall pale-orange candles. A few autumn leaves were strewn down the centre of the table. The only light in the room was from candles, both the ones on the table and those in globe bowls that decorated the sideboard. The shadowy corners seemed brooding to me, but as soon as we sat around the table a formal, slightly forced cheerfulness took hold of us.

Daniel presided over the gathering. Candlelight picked out the gleam in his eye, and his dinner jacket, though slightly large on him, disguised the worst ravages of his illness. He caught me looking at him, winked and tipped his glass to me. I gave a small salute back. Animosity between us did not change the past. Whatever peace with the past I might find would never come from Daniel. That I had realized up on the hill the day before. It wasn't Daniel I needed to forgive, it was myself. That seemed a much harder task.

"Delia, what have you been up to since I saw you last?" Oliver wiped his moustache of crumbs.

"Oh, still a nurse. I do a lot of private care now as well. I was lucky to find my calling as a young person."

Oliver's eyes flicked to Iris, then Daniel and back to me.

"And you, Iris, tell me about you," Lil said. She made it sound like a command. Iris glanced around the table before answering.

"My mother died. I'm looking for a family connection. I think she came from hereabouts."

Lil raised an eyebrow and glanced at Oliver.

"Have you found any?" she asked.

Iris's *not yet* silenced everyone for a moment. Then conversation resumed, as we ran through the issues of the day: would Mary Robinson win the election, how wonderful Nelson Mandela's visit had been, the growing drug trade in the country along with the newfound prosperity that was taking hold. A few glasses of wine later, Lil said to Iris: "But why did you come here? You're Scottish, right?"

"I am. I think I am," Iris said. "My mother said I should look here for relatives. So I came. I believe she sent me to Delia."

Oliver found something fascinating on his fork and Lil leaned forward to look at me.

"Delia? Well, lucky you found her."

"We're happy she did," Daniel said. "Iris is like one of the family, aren't you?"

He smiled benignly, his colour high from wine.

"Family. Isn't that nice? Isn't it?" Lil said to the table at large.

She beamed and looked around the table at us. Other conversations dried up. I tried to make up my mind whether she was truly stupid and unaware of the tension in the room or whether she relished it.

"Why did she send you to Delia?" she asked..

"I don't know, really," Iris said. "I thought maybe Delia knew my mother, but she says not."

Oliver dropped his fork. Jude jumped up and went to find him another. One of the catering staff came in and began to clear the table in preparation for dessert.

"How intriguing," Lil said.

"Your new book will be a hit, as usual," Oliver said to Daniel.

Lil was not put off. She leaned forward to better see me. "And did you know her mother, Delia?"

"I knew a Margaret Butler when I worked in Cardiff," I said. "But she didn't have a child. At least not around the time Iris was born."

"But you were pregnant then," Jude chimed in.

Daniel gave a start.

"What's that, Jude?" he asked. Nobody answered him.

Lil was fairly quivering with excitement. Mike had his hand on Jude's arm. Iris, like Oliver, kept her eyes on her plate. The silence seemed to last forever as I gathered my thoughts.

"I was," I said. "But Iris is not my child. I told you that. Whether any of you believe it or not, it doesn't change the fact. Besides, she didn't come here to find her mother, she came to find relatives. Isn't that right, Iris?"

A blush rose up Jude's neck. Oliver cleared his throat a few times.

"Yes. It is," Iris said. "But since then I've not been able to find any trace of who my mother is, so I'm wondering about that. You must know something, Delia, she sent me to you. You." Iris leaned forward to better see me as she spoke.

"What does she mean, you were pregnant at the time?" Daniel cut in.

No matter my decision to stop as many of the lies as I possibly could, the habit of concealment sealed my throat. I gathered my resolve of the afternoon and tried to speak, but words literally would not come. I took a gulp of wine, cleared my throat and after a moment said as clearly as I could, "She means, when I was in Cardiff I was pregnant. I had a child. Michael John Buckley. He died within a day of being born."

"How did I not know this?" Daniel heaved himself to his feet. "How did I not know?"

"Why should you know? Daniel, sit down, sit down, please," Jude said.

Daniel sank slowly into his chair.

"Why, Delia? Why didn't you tell me you would keep it?"

Jude knocked over her glass of wine. Everyone watched the red stain spread across the tablecloth.

I turned to Iris and spoke only to her.

"With all my heart I wish I could claim a living child. But I can't."

"Daniel, what do you mean? What's going on?" Jude asked.

"It was a long time ago, Jude. A long time, but no use keeping it from you now. Delia and I had an affair. She was pregnant. I thought she was having, you know, something done about it."

"What? When? When did all this happen?"

Nobody answered. Lil absently played with a butter knife, the blade catching the candle glow as it flicked back and forth.

Jude pounded the table with her open hand.

"When, Daniel?"

"The year your mother died." His voice barely carried to the end of the table.

Jude gasped and cried out, "Oh my God. Oh, God."

Mike put his arm around her. She shook him off, stood up and left the dining room. We sat and listened to her steps pound up the stairs.

"Well," Daniel said. "I have some explaining to do tomorrow, but tonight we will enjoy each other's company."

Mike's eyes caught mine. I gave a small shrug. Instinctively I'd known something had to happen in the house soon, but never dreamed it would be this night. Mike shoved his chair back.

"Excuse me, folks. I'm just going to check..." he motioned to the ceiling with his finger.

As soon as the door closed behind him everyone talked at once to restore some normalcy. Eventually, conversation settled on topics like the upcoming election, and gossip about people Oliver, Lil and Daniel knew. Iris leaned towards me and said quietly, "Should I go up to Jude or leave her to Mike?"

"Leave her to Mike," I responded. "I don't think she'll want to see you or me for the moment."

Iris gave me a peculiar look. We all settled in to eat our baked Alaska and make the most of what was left of the dinner without Jude or Mike. Oliver did his best to keep conversation going through the rest of dessert, but he didn't get much help from the rest of us. Lil managed to keep whatever curiosity she had left to herself. It was a relief when Daniel admitted to exhaustion and his need to retire for the night.

"SO TELL ME ABOUT THIS CHILD," DANIEL SAID.

He was settled into bed, propped up by pillows. I smoothed the top of the sheet over the blankets.

"I had a child. He died. What else is there to say?"

"But you were to have an abortion. Isn't that right?"

"No. I was never going to do that. If you knew me at all you would know that. It's not something I could do. I had a son. Our child."

"A boy?" he said, then let out a long breath and sank into his pillows.

"A boy," I said.

"Tell me. Please tell me, Delia."

MY SON WAS BORN PREMATURELY, BY A MONTH. PERHAPS ALL the upset with Maggie and the uncertainty about what to do next affected me, or maybe it was merely bad luck. My blood pressure had soared. The doctor decided to induce. Michael John could have lived, perhaps; many babies did at thirty-two weeks; his chances were fair. He was a small baby to begin with, and as I lay back and waited to hear his first stuttering wail, I feared for him. I waited a long time.

"Is he all right?" I asked.

I raised my head and saw the doctor and two nurses' backs as they worked together, voices low.

"Is he all right?" I said, louder this time. I tried to get off the bed and go see them, but a nurse came and firmly pushed me back on the pillows.

"Give us a minute now," she said. "We're not finished here yet."

As the final business and clean-up after birth took place I heard a small, weak wail.

"There now," one of the nurses said. She didn't smile.

That something was amiss was clear and became clearer as they didn't bring me my son to hold. Instead the doctor came and sat on the edge of my bed.

"He's come early, so he is having a little trouble. He's small."

"Can I hold him? I want to see him, at least."

The nurse wheeled an incubator towards the bed. My son lay there, his little chest filling up and collapsing like a balloon being inexpertly blown. The tubes attached to him looked bigger than he was.

"Will he be all right?"

"We have to wait and see. The birth wore him out. Stay optimistic. The two of you need a bit of rest."

"His colour is not good, not even with the oxygen," I said.

I reached into the incubator. His skin was so soft I felt the roughness of my own would shred it. I touched his hand. His fingers opened and closed on one of mine, the lightest of grips, a fairy's touch, rather than the strong grip of a newborn.

"We'll do our best for him. We will," the doctor said. "We need to get him to the nursery, now. You rest and we'll talk later."

Later I sat in a hard chair in the nursery and held my son with all the tenderness I could muster while the hospital priest baptized him Michael John Buckley, after my father. That he would not survive was clear. He was detached from the tubes and weighed nothing in my arms. I inhaled his newborn scent, kissed his little head, smoothed the fine dark down that covered his skull and whispered love-nonsense to him. He stopped breathing about thirty minutes after the priest left. The nurse came to check on us but I wouldn't let him go. She held me round the shoulders briefly and left us in peace for a while.

We buried him, Adele and I, in the city graveyard.

Later, on my final trip to Cardiff, I had a small headstone put on his grave with a triskele and his name and date of birth and death engraved on it. He had lived one day.

It was not a wonder I lost the child in the end. At first it seemed like punishment for all my sins: Daniel, Ellen, Maggie. Maybe it was as the doctor told me, an unfortunate thing that happened.

I shared none of these thoughts with Daniel.

"I WENT AWAY TO CARDIFF," IS WHAT I TOLD HIM. "I WORKED there. Said I was married and my husband died."

"Does your family know?"

"No. I suppose I will tell them now. Or later. In any event, I don't want them to hear it from anyone else."

"None of us will say a word."

He sounded so certain, but I was long ago finished with believing such assertions. No, I would tell Mam, and deal with whatever happened.

"But what were you going to do? Give it up?"

"It was he. Michael. He was not an it," I said.

"Of course, of course. Forgive me, I'm trying to get used to the idea. Why didn't you tell me before?"

A burst of laughter came from the parlour, followed by the slam of the kitchen door.

"What was the point? It's past and gone, Daniel. Oh, I admit I resented you over the years, but I had my own part in it. One way or the other, it's done."

"You could have told Iris this. She thinks you could be her mother, though she doesn't say it."

"I told her I was not. The rest of it I considered my own business."

"I'm sorry, Delia, for it all. Sorry. I wish you had told me you would go on with the pregnancy. What did you intend to do afterwards?"

"It doesn't matter, Daniel," I said, surprised to find that indeed, in that moment, it did not. "And I did tell you I couldn't have an abortion. You simply didn't want to know that."

"Well, now I have to face Jude in the morning."

He cupped his face in his hands, then dropped them to the bed.

"Simply be honest with her, Daniel. She's grown up now. She's divorced herself, so she knows about human frailty."

"Human frailty indeed."

I gave him his evening meds, then wished him a goodnight.

"Well, not much chance of that," he said.

28

I DITHERED IN THE HALLWAY OUTSIDE HIS ROOM TRYING TO decide whether to go to my room or join the others for a drink in the parlour. Relieved that I didn't have to lie about myself anymore, I knew there was still the matter of Iris to be dealt with. I was about to go back to talk to Daniel about that when Oliver came out of the kitchen with a bottle of wine in hand.

"There you are. Is Daniel all settled in?" he said.

I told him yes. We stood awkwardly there for a second or two.

"Look, let's take this bottle somewhere quiet and chat. There has to be somewhere we can hide out in this mansion."

The invitation brought to me how very tired I was, how much I needed a friend right then. Oliver was not exactly a friend, but he was the closest I had in the moment.

"Has Jude come down? Or Mike?"

"Not yet. Lil is bending Iris's ear in the parlour. I'd be happy to miss that," he said.

"It's a nice enough night. Let's go sit outside."

We donned our coats and slipped out the back door with a bottle of wine and a couple of glasses. At the last moment I grabbed an old blanket from the box by the door. It was a fair night. There was no breeze, though the clouds moved, covering and uncovering stars as they passed. An owl hooted somewhere on the edge of the property.

"Well, that was some dinner conversation," Oliver said as we settled on the bench under the tree. I shrugged.

"I wondered over the years about how you got along since I met you that time in Stephen's Green. I'm sorry you lost the baby."

"Thanks," I said. "It all seems like such a long time ago, but at the same time it seems like yesterday. Meeting Daniel again and ending up nursing him was not in my plans."

"Ah, plans. They are the undoing of us, aren't they?"

I spread the blanket over both of our laps. Some nocturnal beast scurried in the bushes close by.

"What about Iris?"

"Oliver, how much of a scallywag was Daniel in his day? Other women, I mean."

Oliver shuffled his feet, the leather soles of his shoes scraping the small stones causing the rustle in the bushes to stop abruptly.

"He liked to have a good time. I think you are the only one he was in any way serious about."

"Oh, Oliver, don't. You don't have to pretend. I don't think he was serious about me at all. He'd never have left Ellen, would he?"

"Probably not."

We sipped our wine and a tomcat's yowl carried to us from outside the wall. It was, in a way, a relief to hear Oliver say out loud what I'd known and kept inside all along.

"And Iris? Where does she come in?"

I'd been over and over the conversations Adele and I had in Cardiff, searching for clues, for those little ways that we betray what we know.

"I can't say," I replied.

"Can't or won't?"

"What were you, brought up by the Jesuits? It may be possible she's Daniel's daughter."

Oliver whistled. Then grew serious again.

"Daniel is in a terrible state, isn't he?"

There was no point in denying it, so I didn't. Oliver sighed. He poured us each more wine and we sipped in silence.

"Well, I don't suppose he'll make the book launch. It makes me sad, Delia. I've known him a long, long time. If she is his daughter, he ought to know."

A protest rose to my lips, but I squashed it down.

"It's only a possibility. Jude thinks she's Fran's daughter," I said.

"Oh my, now there's a twist. I never thought of that. I do think I see some light family resemblance, but it's not strong. We've all met people who look like people they are not related to. Could she be Fran's?"

This was the easiest question anyone had asked me in weeks.

"No. I'm certain she's not. Fran would never stay away all these years on purpose. Jude wants it to be so, that's all."

"Well, you sound sure of that at least."

"Oh, I am. Whether or not she's Daniel's child I don't know, but I'd bet the farm on the fact that she's not Fran's."

29

OLIVER, LIL AND I MET IN THE KITCHEN FOR BREAKFAST THE next morning, Oliver and I somewhat the worse for wear. Lil bounced in, her energy making us wince as we sat over our plates of bacon and eggs.

"Well, that was an interesting evening," she said as she pulled an extra chair to the table.

Nobody answered. She tucked into her bacon and eggs with gusto.

"Anyone seen Jude today?" I asked.

Nobody had, but she must have been here to lay out the breakfast things. Or perhaps Iris had. I wondered whether or not Mike had stayed upstairs with her. I was glad when it was time to sort Daniel out for the day. On the way to his room I ran into Iris coming down the stairs.

"Have you seen Jude?"

"No, not yet," she said. "I knocked on her door but got no answer. I think she went away with Mike late last night. I'm not sure, but I think so. I was pretty drunk going to bed. I've a head on me today, I can tell you. That Lil talked my ear off and to save my hearing I had a few extra glasses of wine."

She hesitated, made to speak. Stopped herself.

Before she could say anything about last night, I said: "Look, I've got a trip out to Curraghchase planned for tomorrow. It's beautiful there, a lovely forest park, quite unspoiled. I'd like you to come. There's someone I'd like you to meet. I remember how much you liked being out in the wilds after your mother died."

She looked astounded, and I suppose I couldn't blame her. I had thought about how to extend the invitation, and blurting it out that morning was not what I had intended.

"Sure. Yeah. Let's do that. I've nothing on anyway and I've not been out there. I thought you'd be away to see Maggie on your day off."

"Ah, the Cork-Kilkenny hurling final is on at Croke Park. Dublin will be mental. A day in the country is exactly what I need. Clear my head after all this revelry."

⚭.

"IS JUDE UP?" DANIEL ASKED AS SOON I POKED MY NOSE INTO HIS room. I told him she was out, likely with Mike.

"Well, I need to get up now anyway. I want to see Oliver and Lil before they go."

Despite the effort it was for him to get out of bed, he wouldn't entertain at all the idea of visitors coming to his room. He leaned heavily on me as we made our way to the parlour.

Lil and Oliver were there already. Lil was examining the photos on the mantel. Oliver put down the paper and took Daniel's other arm, so I handed Daniel off to him and went to the kitchen. My head was still aching from too much wine, and my stomach was in knots at the idea of facing Jude whenever she turned up. I left them to it and went to get another cup of tea.

Iris was in the kitchen clearing up after breakfast.

"Any word from Jude yet?" I asked.

"No. I guess she needs some time to absorb what she heard last night. I had no idea you and Daniel saw each other at one time. And I'm sorry you lost your son. I really am. I guess we should have minded our own business. It's just that you were always so mysterious. Anyway, I had kind of hoped you were related to me, you know."

"Why, thank you, Iris."

God knows I'd given her no reason to hope that. I was so touched and surprised I almost forgot my worry about Jude and talking to Mam before she heard any gossip. Not that I thought anyone would deliberately spread the word, but in a small place like Kiltilly the very walls have ears.

"Well, I suppose we should show our faces in the parlour to be polite," Iris said.

BY NOON LIL HAD LEFT FOR DUBLIN AND NEITHER JUDE NOR Mike had shown up. Oliver kept Daniel engaged in conversation while Iris and I scoured the kitchen for the makings of lunch. We were all wilted and keyed up at the same time. It crossed my mind that unburdening myself of my own secrets hadn't helped anything at all. I said as much to Iris.

"Ah, it will. Jude will come around. She's probably as desperately hungover as the rest of us, that's all."

Daniel ate nothing. He sat like a rag in his chair and let us talk around him. He dropped off to sleep at one point, then woke after a few minutes with a start.

"Is she back?" he asked.

She wasn't. I insisted he go to bed.

"Wearing yourself out won't make her come sooner than she's ready," I told him.

She still wasn't home when the relief nurse came. My nerves were jumping as I handed over to the nurse, said goodbye to Oliver, and left for my day off.

30

IT WAS A LOVELY TIME OF YEAR TO VISIT CURRAGHCHASE. THE trees were decked out in yellow, brown and orange and the paths echoed them, though a little soggy from recent rains. Iris was enchanted by the pair of swans that paddled up to the edge of the pond, wings up, eyes alert.

"Iris, I haven't been entirely truthful with you about your mother, or who I believe is your mother."

Iris wheeled around to face me and almost lost her footing and fell into the pond. I grabbed her arm to steady her. Bramblings and chaffinches tweeted and twittered nearby.

"My mother?" she said finally.

"Yes."

She looked out over the lake, then walked away a few steps, turned around and came back at me so fast I had to step aside so we didn't collide.

"You knew about my mother all along? And you said nothing?"

"Let's walk. There's someone I want you to meet and we'll be late. I'll tell you what I can as we go."

Originally owned by the poet Sir Aubrey de Vere, Curraghchase was a calm and lovely place of forest, lakes, meadows. De Vere's old mansion still stood and the steps up to it were a fine place to sit and talk privately. I had no illusions that this could turn out to be a very uncalm talk, and as nature always calms me, as it seemed to Iris, this place had come to mind. It was also almost certain that we could talk in complete privacy. We walked down a path patchworked with fallen leaves, the scent of damp decay in our noses, and a wonder of birdsong in our ears. I may as well have been on the moon for all the notice I took of it.

Iris listened as I described meeting Adele on the ferry to Cardiff, how we forged our friendship out of loneliness and similar situations. I told her nothing of Daniel or Jimmy McCann. Yet.

"Maggie was supposed to take my child and raise it as her own, but she got sick. Adele was such a great support to me then. We were still working out what to do when I had to be induced and my child, Michael, died. I'd never have got through it without Adele. And I was there for her when her child was born."

I've never been a smoker, yet for some reason I wished I had the excuse of lighting up just then. I could have done with the break, because the hard part of the story was coming.

"Adele was afraid of a man she'd been going out with in Ireland before. He was a violent and terrible man who stalked her. She wanted to be sure he would never find her and especially that he should know nothing about her child. She wanted to protect herself and her child. Her sister put her in touch with a friend, Margaret Butler, who was about to immigrate to Australia. Peg Butler had no intention of coming back to Ireland, so we got her UK identification, including her National Insurance Number, and when Peg left, Adele became Maggie Butler and moved away with her baby. She told nobody where she went."

"Your friend Adele is my mother?"

"I believe so. You have similar eyes to hers."

Iris took a few deep breaths. A pair of mallards skimmed the treetops, and blackbirds' yellow beaks glinted from the bushes as we passed.

"But you're not sure?"

"I'm not certain sure. It's likely. We agreed that if anything happened to her while you were small she would send me word. She wanted me to look out for you, keep you safe if she couldn't. I never expected you to turn up a grown woman."

"Why didn't you tell me? Why?"

Shame made me cringe. All Adele and I went through filled me with sadness. We lived in an unfortunate time and did the best we could within it. Twenty-two years later the world had changed, and our choices might seem quaint and shameful. Mam was right. We were indeed second-class citizens with a list of rules that allowed no error if we were to keep our good name, and our good name meant more than behaving decently.

"It was complicated for me, Iris. That's all I can say. And I did want to keep my promise to your mother to keep you safe."

"Safe? How was I not safe?"

The house came into view atop the hill. A figure in a bright blue coat paced the courtyard dwarfed by the edifice. I steered us in that direction.

"Adele believed the man she ran from would harm her and possibly you. She wanted to keep him well away from you. Iris, I'm taking you to meet someone. If Adele is your mother, Leigh is your aunt." I gestured toward the figure on the steps.

"My aunt? I can't take this in."

She grabbed her head, her eyes wide, and exhaled a long, loud breath. We approached the base of the steps. I waved at Leigh, who waved back, then began to descend the steps.

"I think I'm angry," Iris said.

She stopped walking. I thought she was going to run away, so I took her arm and moved her forward. Leigh met us halfway down the steps.

"Iris, this is Leigh, Adele's sister. Leigh, I do believe this is Adele's daughter."

They hesitated as they took each other in. Their curiosity made them reserved. After they said their hellos we walked back up and sat on the low wall. When I phoned Leigh after my evening on the hill I had told her the gist of things and arranged this meeting.

"I'm sorry to hear about your mother," Leigh said.

After some awkward chat she took out the photos she'd brought of Adele.

"Look at these, pet. Is this your mam?" Leigh offered the photos.

Iris reached out to take them, then put her hands back on her lap, knotting her fingers.

"Iris?" I said.

"I'm afraid it won't be her," she said quietly.

Leigh took Iris's hand and put the photos in them.

"Only one way to know, pet," she said. "Isn't knowing better than not knowing?"

Iris held the photos a moment, then turned over first one, then the next, until she'd seen all three. She nodded without raising her head.

"Yes. It's her. It's my mum."

THEY TALKED UNTIL THE EVENING CHILL SET IN, LEIGH NAMING aunties and uncles, cousins, grandmothers and grandfathers alive and dead. Iris told stories of growing up and her life with Adele. Tears were shed at the loss of Adele and the lost years that lay between them. By the time their talk ran down I was chilled practically to the bone. There was one more thing I had to do before we turned for home.

"Iris, I have something else for you here, now I know for sure it's you."

Having no idea what I would say to her if she asked about her father, yet determined I would tell no more lies, I handed her a folded paper. I waited as she unfolded the copy of her long-form birth certificate. The real one that registered her actual birth in Cardiff, showing her name as Iris Sweeney.

"But, I have a short-form birth certificate in my name. I mean Iris Butler. How can there be two?" Iris was even more confused that she had been earlier.

"That's a fake. I have no idea how Adele pulled that off, but it is a fake. We had someone make it so Jimmy couldn't trace Adele at all. If anyone official examined it closely, you'd be done for."

"God, so much trouble you all went to. Is Jimmy that bad?"

"Oh, he is and worse," Leigh said. "But we'll just have to deal with that if he comes back and makes trouble."

Iris took that in silence. If we didn't move soon I'd lose the use of my legs. Finally, she asked the question she had to ask and I had been dreading.

"It says here 'father unknown.' Is this Jimmy my father?"

"Probably," Leigh said. "Maybe," I said. We spoke at the same time.

Iris looked from one of us to the other, and Leigh said, "What do you mean, maybe? Do you know something I don't?"

"It was between Jimmy and another man. Adele told me she didn't which one was the father. So..." I shrugged.

"I just don't know what to believe anymore," Iris said.

Tense and teary, she turned her back on Leigh and me and hunched into her jacket. Leigh looked at me, eyebrows raised. I shrugged again.

Before I came out here to introduce Iris to Leigh and tell her all I knew, I had made up my mind not to tell her about Daniel unless she asked specifically for names of men who might be her father. She would ask sooner or later, that I knew, yet in my heart I hoped she wouldn't. Pride, I suppose. I didn't want to admit just how gullible and deceived I'd been by Daniel. The truth was, in spite of my feelings for Daniel being as dead as it was possible for them to be, it still hurt that he'd thought so little of me back then. It was a marvel that Adele and I had developed a friendship, but that was a tribute to Adele. When it became clear that Maggie would not be able to take care of my child, Adele persuaded me to keep him, that together we could support each other and our babies. I was to abscond with her, get a job as a nurse wherever we settled, and we would share responsibilities for our children. The thought of never going back to Kiltilly to live, of deceiving my parents forever, galled me, but the chance of keeping Michael was too good to pass up. When Michael died, Adele let me out of the promise. Instead she asked that if anything happened to her I would make sure that Iris stayed out of the clutches of Jimmy McCann. I had promised. It was not only self-interest that stopped me telling what I knew before this.

Iris broke into my thoughts. "Who were they, these men my mother thought might be my father?"

I took a deep breath.

"Jimmy McCann was one," I said. "The other was Daniel Wolfe."

"Daniel Wolfe," she and Leigh said together.

Heat of humiliation rose in my face. I held my voice steady as I answered, "Yes."

"Jesus, who would've guessed that," Leigh said.

A desperate need to move came over me, and it was not just the cold creeping from the broken cement through my thin leather-soled shoes. If I was supposed to feel better after telling the truth, I was failing miserably. And after this I'd have to find a way to talk to Mam. And soon.

"You mean, I am a half-sister to Jude?"

"Possibly."

"And, if your son had lived, I'd be a half-sister to him too, right?"

I nodded again.

"Oh my God. I can't get my head around this. I just can't."

Iris began to pace back and forth, her hands buried deep in her pockets. The piercing cry of a sparrow hawk sounded from overhead.

"Does Jude know any of this?" she asked as she swished by me, turned and took off again without waiting for a reply. When she came back round I told her no.

"Well, what will we say to her?" Iris asked.

"Right now I've no idea," I said. "But your father could be Jimmy and not Daniel at all. And I'm frozen. Let's go into Adare and have something to heat us up. We'll figure it out then."

31

IRIS WAS QUIET ON THE DRIVE BACK, WHICH SUITED ME just fine, as I was preoccupied with the prospect of meeting Jude. In my heart I hoped that news that Iris might be her half-sister would dilute the impact of my affair with Daniel. I wasn't at all sure it would. We dropped off my car at the farm but didn't have time to stay for tea, as I was due back on duty in about an hour.

The sky was darkening to dusk as we walked towards Daniel's. I listened to the tap of my heels and the scuffle of Iris's boots as I searched for any remnant of the peace and joy I used to experience on this road not so long ago. Life, it seemed, had narrowed down to memories of the past and tensions of the present.

"Do you think Daniel is my father?" Iris asked.

"I don't know. Adele told me she didn't know."

"But what do you think?"

How many times had I asked myself that question since Iris showed up on Daniel's doorstep? Twenty-two years ago I had persuaded myself that Adele's child was not Daniel's. Wishful thinking, perhaps. Or maybe Adele's insouciance about it rubbed off on me. At any rate, I'd held on to that belief all through the years, only to have the whole question reopened these last months.

"I really don't know," I told Iris.

Iris sighed. We stepped to the side of the road out of the wash of wet leaves and puddle spray as a van passed us, then we continued on, each lost in our own thoughts. At the village edge Iris stopped. I stood with her as the streetlights came on, soft yellow halos in the dusk.

"I hope Jude won't be angry with me," Iris said.

"Why on earth would she be angry with you?" I was genuinely surprised.

She shrugged and turned away. We stood together at the village crossroads. I ached to hold her; perhaps she ached to be held; yet paralyzed and undone by the tenderness I felt towards her, I couldn't do it.

"Oh, just because. You know, I may be proof her father is not who she thinks he is."

I did put my arm around her then. She rested her head against me.

"That's not your fault, pet. You are innocent in that. Jude will understand that. She will."

THE RELIEF NURSE REPORTED THAT DANIEL HAD STAYED IN BED all day and Jude hadn't returned home. When I looked in on him, Daniel was propped up on pillows sleeping. I withdrew and shut the door as gently as I could. Iris was still in the hallway where I had left her.

"Well, I guess we have to wait," I said to her.

"I'll die of nerves, I really will."

"It's not so easy to die."

No sooner were the words out of my mouth than we heard a key turning in the front-door lock. We stood together, rooted to the spot, as the door swung open. Jude came in. None of the three of us moved for a moment; then Iris said, "Jude, I'm so glad you're back."

Jude turned from us and shut the door without answering. Iris raised her eyebrows at me. It seemed to me then that I should speak to Jude privately before breaking the news to her; try to get back on some less awkward footing than the cool avoidance we'd been engaged in and which was now open hostility.

"Jude, can we talk?" I said.

"I have nothing to say to you," Jude answered without looking at me.

"We, Iris and I, have some things to say to you and Daniel together. But I would like a word with you first, if you are willing."

Jude slowly shrugged off her coat and hung it on the coat tree with exaggerated care, smoothing her scarf over the collar of it before she turned to face us again. She looked tired and pale.

"I want to speak to my father alone," she said.

I told her he was sleeping.

"What? You can't stop me speaking to my own father."

"Jude, that's unfair," Iris said.

We still stood outside Daniel's door. I started for the kitchen at the same time Jude began to walk towards us. Not wanting to pass close to her, I changed my mind and went into the parlour, desperate to sit down because my legs had begun to shake. Through the open door I heard Iris say, "Are you okay, Jude? We've all been worried about you."

Jude didn't answer. A nearby door opened, then closed again almost immediately. Her voice came to me from the hallway. Presumably she had discovered that Daniel was indeed sleeping.

"What is that you and Delia want to talk about?"

"It's... We should wait. We want to talk to both you and Daniel together. It's better that way."

"So you and Delia have something to say about my father, is that it?"

The sneer in her voice was ugly. I went back out to protest the way she spoke to Iris, but just then Daniel's bell rang. Jude stopped me outside his door.

"Leave him alone. I'll go see what he wants."

She flounced into Daniel's room, leaving Iris and me in the hallway. Moments later she was back.

"Daniel wants to see you, Delia," she said. She avoided looking at me and simply brushed by me and went upstairs.

"Don't worry, pet, we'll work it out," I said to Iris, though I was not at all sure how.

"Thank God you're back," Daniel said when I entered. "And Jude, too. We have to face her together, Delia. I let you down once, and I'll not do it again."

I hadn't the heart to tell him he couldn't let me down anymore. Not in any way.

"Daniel, Iris and I want to talk to you and Jude together. When you're up for it. Maybe we can sort it all out then, maybe we can't. In any event, none of us can change the past."

"Help me up, help me up now, we'll get this done tonight. I need it done, Delia. I don't think I've got a lot left in me. Certainly not for all this fighting with Jude. I just don't have the heart for it. Why you and Iris? What does Iris have to do with it?"

"Let's wait till we talk. Are you sure you're able to get up?"

"Yes, yes. Hurry, before Jude disappears again. She's none too pleased with any of us. Let's get it sorted out now before it goes any further."

&

DANIEL AND JUDE LISTENED IN SILENCE WHILE I TOLD THEM about Adele. When I'd finished, the silence dragged on for what seemed like hours. Iris shifted in her chair, leaned forward as if about to speak, then sat back again. Jude kept her eyes fixed on the wall in front of her. Daniel cleared his throat twice then spoke.

"Adele? I don't remember an Adele."

Iris held out the photo Leigh had given her. Daniel took it and examined it a moment. Then he smiled.

"Ah, Addie. Addie worked in my bank. I met her there. But I never made her pregnant. I'd stake my life on that. I couldn't have."

Jude snorted and jerked as if she'd been burned.

"So you got two women pregnant at the same time. How many brothers and sisters do I actually have, potentially?"

"It's not like that, Jude. I was no saint, but I didn't just go around making women pregnant. I'm sure I never made Addie pregnant. I knew her from the bank. We had tea a few times, that's all."

Iris's eyes caught mine. I shrugged.

"Did Fran know about your affair with Delia? Did she know you were out on the town with everyone and anyone while Mother was here looking after the house, and us, and the whole bloody estate? Did she?"

"Not as far as I know. And I wasn't running around with everyone and anyone. I didn't have an affair with Addie. I was involved with Delia then."

Daniel's voice was barely above a whisper. It should have pleased me to see him made to answer for himself, but it didn't.

"And what about Delia? Did Mother know about her? About the two of you?"

"Your mother did. I spoke to her when Delia became pregnant. Fran knew nothing, as far as I know."

Jude snorted again. Before she could say anything else, Iris spoke up. "My mother told Delia you could be my father."

Daniel threw up his hands, then began to cough. I got him a glass of water. A light sheen of sweat emphasized the grey colour of his face.

"I knew your mother," Daniel said to Iris when he got his breath back. "I liked her. She was a lovely girl. I did give her money to get away from some gurrier. I did do that. In fact, I drove her to the ferry when she left. It was only luck we didn't run into each other on the dock, Delia."

"How can you remember all that and not know if you had sex with her?" Jude asked.

"I do know. There was nothing like that between us at all. Not at all."

Conversations with Adele flashed through my mind. Distinctly she'd said that Daniel could be her child's father. Maybe it was not simply my not wanting it to be true; maybe Adele was not being honest.

"Tell me again, Delia. Adele said that Daniel could be the father, right?" Jude asked.

"She said that, yes. But she was desperate to protect herself and her baby from Jimmy McCann. She might have just said it. Maybe it wasn't true. I don't know."

Jude got up and stood by the window, her back to us. Daniel coughed again, just once, the sound harsh in the silence.

"It's just all too much. Mother died that year and Fran vanished. It must have something to do with all this."

Jude didn't turn around as she spoke. Iris half rose from her chair then sat back again. I thought longingly of a cup of tea. Or something stronger.

"I told your mother about Delia a week before the accident. She didn't die because of that; she knew I was...she knew I was away a lot and that there were occasionally other women. We had an understanding. We did, Jude. She died because it was an accident. It was winter. The road was slippery. Fran went months later for her own reasons, maybe. Maybe something happened to her we have never discovered. There was no connection at all."

I did get up then and pour a drink from the decanter on the sideboard. I offered one to the others, but only Daniel accepted. Whiskey slopped onto the carpet as I poured for him. I rubbed it into the pile with my foot.

"Jude, don't judge too harshly. It was all a long time ago. It's done. We've all suffered enough," Daniel said.

Jude came back and sat down in the wing chair by the fireplace where she could see us all. "Well, there's one part of this we can clear up. If you, Iris, and you, Daniel, would agree to a paternity test, it would settle one thing. Wouldn't it?"

"Yes. Yes, of course," Iris said.

Jude turned to Daniel.

"Much as I would be happy to have you as a daughter, Iris, I am certain you aren't mine. Let's do the test and lay this to rest," said Daniel.

"I really thought, hoped, you were Fran's child," Jude said to Iris, her voice shaky with tears. "Now you might be my sister. It's just..."

She stopped talking and blew her nose. I wanted to say again that Iris was not Fran's child, but there seemed no point in it. I'd been saying so ever since Iris showed up, to no avail. Besides, I was digesting the news that Daniel had talked to Ellen about my pregnancy and his assertion that Iris could not be his daughter.

32

ORGANIZING THE PATERNITY TEST THAWED OUT THE atmosphere between Jude and Daniel a little. Jude had arranged for his doctor to come to take blood from both her father and Iris, and stood over them while it was done.

"Well, that's that," Daniel said when it was all over. "We'll know for sure when we get the results."

"You'll not know for sure exactly unless you are no relation to each other," his doctor said. "They're making great strides in this, but it's no exact science yet. Still, you'll know if you could be and if you couldn't. That's good enough."

Jude, I guessed, wanted something more solid, but Dr. Reilly wasn't giving it to her. When we were alone outside the room, he shook his head.

"I'm not sure he'll be around for the results," Dr. Reilly said when we were alone. "All this excitement is wearing him out."

It was. By the end of that week he was no longer getting up out of bed at all. Jude spent hours with him; the murmur of voices as they talked or she read to him became part of the creaks and background noises of the house. The crackle of tension showed in the overly polite interactions between Jude and me. We avoided each other as much as possible. In spite of Daniel's prior assurance I worried what would happen with the farm mortgage when Jude was in charge. Iris picked up more shifts at the café to keep herself busy. Her daily runs got longer and she sang less around the house. Daniel stayed in his room, most days not even making it as far as his chair. So we all waited to learn the secrets of Iris and Daniel's blood.

33

MAGGIE WAS IN HER CHAIR IN THE CORNER OF HER ROOM with her eyes closed. She had sat up a bit when we came in but didn't interact with us at all, in spite of Mam and me trying to draw her out. I wondered if she was unwell and talked to the nurse in charge, who said that she was just quieter these days due to a change in medication. I couldn't make up my mind whether it was a good thing or not. She was calmer, for sure, but seemed more withdrawn. For once her hair was unsnarled and tidy. I tried to coax her to walk down the corridor with us, but she wasn't having any of it. She perked up when Mam gave her the sweets Da had sent. No mention was made of the baby, much to my relief.

"She should have stayed in the nuns," Mam said.

"Ah, Mam, she wasn't cut out to be a nun, that's why she was asked to leave."

Mam picked up the hairbrush and put it down again, at a loss to have nothing to fuss over with Maggie.

TUCKED INTO A CORNER TABLE IN AN ALMOST EMPTY SECTION of the tearoom, we sat across from each other at Bewley's with our usual cuppa and bite to eat after we left St. Mary's. It was the fourth time I'd seen Mam on my own since Daniel's dinner party and I still hadn't told her anything about my pregnancy. Three afternoons while Jude sat with Daniel I had walked out to the farm, resolved I'd talk to Mam and Da, but I had backed out every time. There was no shortage of excuses I came up with: I was wrung out from the confrontation with Jude, I didn't have time, I wanted to talk to them separately and they were never apart. All excuses. My parents were proud of me. I'd done well in life. I stayed in the village when I could have gone to a bigger city or emigrated to make more money. I'd helped out on the farm as my father aged. I'd been a good daughter. It was hard to disappoint them. Besides, I'd not decided whether or not to tell them it was Daniel I'd been involved with. They were beholden to him for the farm and I couldn't see that sitting well with them.

The last time I'd been out there, a few days ago, I'd steeled myself to tell them. Mam was making apple tarts when I arrived. The front of her apron was streaked with flour and her tongue hung on the corner of her mouth as she chopped margarine through flour, the pair of knives she used clicking against each other almost in time to the tick of the clock.

"Too bad that won't be ready before I go," I said.

"I'll save you a bit," she said and sprinkled flour onto the counter before turning out the mixture from the bowl.

I almost told her then, but the sight of her going about baking a pie, as I'd seen her do every week or so for my whole life, stopped the words on my tongue. For something to do I filled the kettle and put it on the hob. By the time it boiled Mam had the top crust on the pie. She held it up with one hand as she trimmed the excess off. The shorn pieces fell to the counter in a limp heap.

"Call your father for a cuppa," Mam said.

So I did, and took the cowardly way out again.

"DELIA, ARE YOU LISTENING TO ME?" MAM'S VOICE BROUGHT ME back to Bewley's. "Doesn't Maggie seem more away with the fairies since her operation? She talks a lot less. Have you noticed?"

I had noticed. We talked all around it for a while. Mam, as usual, trying to see some improvement in Maggie.

"As long as she's safe and as happy as she can be, that's all we can ask for," I said.

"Well, we can only believe that." Mam sighed. "Ah, Delia, at least we have you. You've always been a good daughter. Never given us a day's trouble."

Mam patted my arm as she spoke. My eyes filled. Before I could stop or hide them, a few tears plopped onto the table.

"What is it, Delia, what's up?" Mam said.

It was impossible to look her in the eye so I kept my eyes down.

"Delia, tell me what's wrong. You can talk to me."

For a wild second I thought of claiming fatigue, or worry for Maggie, but in the end I knew the time had come to tell my tale.

"I'm not such a good daughter. Not like you think."

When I finally looked up, Mam had her cup halfway to her mouth. She put it back on the saucer.

"What do you mean, Delia? Have you done something?"

"Yes, I have. I have. It was a long time ago, though. I'm telling you now so you won't hear it anywhere else."

"So, what is it? What's got you this upset?"

I told her almost everything, about being left pregnant, about Maggie agreeing to take the baby and meeting Adele. I told her the baby had died. I didn't say that Daniel had anything to do with the whole mess.

"God, Delia, if I hadn't heard it from your mouth I wouldn't have believed it," she said when I'd finished. "Was it some lad from the village? Was it Daniel Wolfe? Is that what he has to do with all this?"

"Mam, it doesn't matter who it was. Really. It was years ago. I was stupid. That's all."

Mam took a sip of tea and made a face.

"It's cold," she said. "I can't drink that."

I caught the waitress's eye and asked for a hot pot. Mam ran her hand across her mouth several times, her eyes looking for something to settle on in the room. The waitress came back with a fresh pot of tea.

"So why are you bringing this up now, after all these years?" Mam asked when we were alone again.

"Because Iris went to Cardiff to find out about her mother and someone who knew me there told her that I was expecting. I lied to everyone when I went, said I was married. You know how it is, once someone gets a handle on a story, soon everyone knows. I just don't want you hearing about it from anyone but me. I'll tell Da as soon as we get back."

"Don't you worry about that, I'll tell him. What he'll make of it, God knows."

She poured tea for herself, put in milk and sugar. She stirred for about a full minute, the spoon clinking round the cup faster and faster. I touched her hand to stop it.

"Mam, drink it while it's hot. No need for you to tell Da, it's best I tell him myself."

"Does everyone at the Big House know all this?"

"Yes."

Without looking at me she patted my hand.

"Jesus, girl, it was terrible that you went through all that alone. Why didn't you tell us?"

"Because you'd have had a kitten. You know you would."

She slurped her tea, then nodded.

"Aye, right enough. Times were different then, but we'd have gotten over it, you know. Just like your da will when you tell him. Eventually, he'll get over it."

My fear was, of course, that he wouldn't, as he never got over Maggie's trouble. I said as much as to Mam.

"That's different entirely. Tell me, is the baby Maggie goes on about this one of yours?"

"Probably. She was so looking forward to having a child to care for."

"Is that what happened? When you lost the child she went strange?"

She hardly let me finish speaking before the question tumbled out of her mouth. Guilt and the urge to comfort her competed in me for a moment. One thing I'd learned this past summer was that my anger and resentment at Daniel allowed me to forget that it was not just my and Maggie's lives that were so sadly affected by my decision to keep the baby. I was not now going to add to my mother's troubles.

"Ah, Mam, no. Sure Maggie was already in the home when Michael died."

"Ah well. Maggie always wanted to have children. I know that. That's why she left the convent, no matter that the nuns say she was unstable. Did you know that?"

"I did. But I don't think the convent would have suited her anyway. She was too independent."

"Well, that didn't get her far, did it? She'd probably have been better off to take the veil. We'll never know."

She put her hand over her mouth, but not before I'd seen her lip tremble. Not for the first time I wished I could turn back time and, if I couldn't resist Daniel Wolfe, at least I could have had the courage to go against the Church. Surely living with that would have been less painful and a lot less destructive to everyone than all that happened because I stood by what my faith demanded. But as Mam said: we'll never know.

WE GOT BACK TO THE FARM AT MILKING TIME, SO I TOLD DA IN the barn. He kept his hands moving on the teats and the milk rattled into the bucket before settling into a quieter hiss as the level of milk rose. When I finished he leaned into the cow's flank for a moment. I waited out the silence.

"Well, that's a story," he said finally. "Poor lass, but you're a silly girl letting some fellow take advantage of you. Not the way we brought you up."

"Well, at least you won't hear it from someone else," I said.

He rose from the stool, arms straight by his sides as we faced each other.

"Aye. There's that. Thanks for that."

"Da," I said. "I'm sorry."

He took off his cap and settled it back on his head the way he always did surveying the situation when the animals were sick, or a crop was lost.

"Well, what's done is done. As long as you are all right now, we'll speak no more of it."

I moved to hug him, but he turned and sat back down on his stool by the next cow. I listened to the milk fill the bucket for a minute and then left. As Mam said, it would take time.

34

THE LETTERBOX OPENED AND CLOSED WITH A CLACK. Daniel and I froze.

"That's probably it," Daniel said.

We had been expecting the results of the paternity test for days. This day Jude was out with Mike instead of hovering around the hallway as she had done every day for a few weeks around post time. Iris was at work in the café.

"Go check, go check," Daniel urged.

He sucked his teeth with impatience as I finished rubbing lotion into his feet.

There were three envelopes on the mat. One of them was addressed to Daniel from the outfit that had done the test.

"Well?" he said.

"It's here."

He shook the envelope like it was a gift box, held it up to the light trying to read right though the envelope, then let it rest in his hand on the bedcovers.

"Will you wait till they come back to open it?" I asked.

"I should, I suppose. I don't know. What do you think?"

"Don't ask me. I'm in trouble enough with Jude. This has to be your decision."

He made a face at me, then lifted the envelope again. He passed his thumbs across the paper a few times.

"I know it. Get me up, get me up. I can't look at this from my bed. Suppose she is related to me? What if Jude's right and she's Fran's?"

"At least you'll know that," I said.

We didn't make it to the parlour. By the time he was dressed in a shirt and jacket he was exhausted, so he sat in the easy chair in his room, his pajama bottoms covered with a rug.

"When will they be back?" he asked for the umpteenth time.

"Iris will be a few more hours. Jude, well, I don't know."

"Well, it's addressed to me now, isn't it?"

He slid his thumb under the edge of the flap. His resolve to wait had lasted all of ten minutes since getting to his chair. He unfolded the single sheet of paper. The clock from the kitchen chimed the hour and crows proclaimed their presence from the trees outside as he read through it.

"Well, there it is, Delia. There it is."

He handed the page to me.

"SO MAYBE YOU ARE RIGHT, DELIA. MAM JUST WANTED TO PUT everyone off the scent."

The four of us were in Daniel's room digesting the test result, which gave a negligible probability of a blood relationship between Iris and Daniel.

"I only thought that later," I said. "At first I thought it was probably true that he was."

Daniel protested. I shrugged at him.

"I never really thought of Daniel being her father," Jude said. "I thought Fran was her mother."

"Well, I'm glad my memory is not at fault, anyway," Daniel said. "Though I would have been very proud to claim you as a daughter, Iris. Or a grandchild, come to that."

"Aw, Daniel, thanks."

Iris kissed him on the head. He caught her hand in his and planted a kiss on it.

"That makes my father a drug-running, murdering criminal then," Iris said.

"Well," Daniel said, "your choices were not stellar in any event."

Iris's laugh infected us, or maybe relief that the matter was settled. We all began to talk at once.

"Well, let's have a drink then," Daniel said.

Jude poured a generous portion of whiskey for each of us. Daniel raised his glass.

"Here's to life in all its surprises and messy details."

Suddenly sober, we raised our glasses.

"Life," we said in chorus.

&

DANIEL STOPPED MY HAND AS I MOVED THE THERMOMETER towards his mouth.

"Leave it, Delia," he said. "What does it matter at this stage? Sit down."

He patted the bed next to him. He was flushed after the whiskey and excitement of the day. He sank into the pillows and closed his eyes, keeping hold of my hand.

"What must you have thought of me when Adele told you her story?" he said without opening his eyes.

I said nothing, just patted the hand that held mine. We stayed like that a moment, Daniel sunk into his pillow grasping my hand and me patting his.

"Well," he said finally, "at least I've taken care of you now. You'll be all right."

He opened his eyes and tried to sit up. He couldn't hoist himself so he resettled on the pillows.

"I left you the farm free and clear, Delia. It's yours when I'm gone."

At first I couldn't take in what he said. When I did I was almost overcome with gratitude and relief.

"Oh, Daniel, thank you. Thanks."

"It was my intention from the start. I'm glad you are here, Delia. Dealing with all this would have been much harder without you."

Unclear whether he was talking about Jude, Iris, his illness or, more probably, all three, I nonetheless felt some shame that I had held back what I knew, and didn't mention that if I weren't here it probably wouldn't have arisen in the first place.

"I'm sorry, Daniel. I should have said something sooner about Adele."

"None of us are angels, are we? It's all right now. I don't suppose you've changed your mind about helping me over the threshold, have you?"

It would have been so easy, he was that weak physically. Just a nudge too much of morphine.

"Ah, Daniel, no. I can't do that. Are you in pain? It's almost time for your next dose."

He gave a small laugh.

"Pain? Not physical. I'm just bone weary and ready to go."

Later that night I went to his room, the extra dose ready to hand. He was asleep, lying back in bed so still he could have been dead already. His hair had turned whiter these past months. The few darker ones he still had stood in contrast against the grey on the light green pillow sham upon which he rested his head. He looked impossibly fragile and vulnerable. Perhaps this was what made me fall for him in the first place, this ability he had to be successful and confident on the one hand and so unsure of himself on the other, so revealing of his flaws. Grief washed over me then, for the girl I had been and the woman I'd become. Grief for Daniel and Jude, for Maggie, too. Had I really done the right thing all those years ago? On the farm I would kill without qualm a suffering animal that had no hope of a cure.

Daniel muttered something I couldn't catch, then opened his eyes.

"Delia," he said, "you're here."

"Yes, I'm here."

I put the morphine back in my pocket and held his hand.

35

AT ABOUT HALF-PAST TWO IN THE MORNING I GAVE UP TRYING
to sleep and went downstairs to get a cup of tea. A light under the
kitchen door surprised me. Jude was at the table with a finger of
whiskey and the photo of Fran in her green tartan coat and red
and green scarf in front of her. She glanced at me, then turned
back to contemplate the photo without a word. I filled the kettle
and put it on. Neither of us spoke while the kettle roiled and
bubbled. I made my cuppa and was about to take it to my room
when I heard Jude sniffle.

"Everything all right?" I asked.

She wiped her nose on the back of her hand then began to cry
in earnest.

"Ah, Jude. Talk to me."

I grabbed a box of tissues and put them in front of her, then sat
and waited. She took a handful and swiped at her face. She blew
her nose and finally looked at me directly.

"Oh, God, I should be happy for Iris, shouldn't I?" she said.

"Well, it's good she knows now who both her parents are. And
she has discovered aunties and a grandmother."

She emptied her glass and refilled it. "Well, I really thought she
was Fran's daughter. Oh, I know, I know, you warned me. I was so
sure. She laughs like her. She has almost the same singing voice.
I was so sure."

"We see what we want to," I said.

God knows I had.

"It was so much what I wanted. It really was. I have to let Fran go, don't I? Daniel's been telling me that all along. I thought I had, too, but I was wrong. Daniel will be dead soon, and then it will be just me. This isn't what was meant to happen. It's not."

She blew her nose again and wiped her eyes with the cuff of her dressing gown.

"No. But you have a good friend in Iris. You've got that. And Mike. You have him too."

She sat a little straighter in the chair and nodded. The whiskey in the glass shimmied to the shake in her hand. I sipped my tea.

"I so wanted her to be Fran's," she repeated. "To know what happened to Fran. You know? Just to know. I thought it was all connected — Mam's death, Fran going, Iris showing up just as Daniel was ill."

She stroked Fran's image, her fingers trying to find answers. My heart ached for her. In that moment I should have held her, comforted her. I didn't think she'd let me. Neither would my own sense of guilt. I got a glass from the cupboard. Jude passed me the bottle, a small gesture, but the first nearly friendly one she'd made to me lately. I poured myself a shot.

I'D COME FROM CARDIFF TO VISIT MAGGIE FOR THE WEEKEND. Although the day was cold and blustery, I needed to get out, away from buildings, from the packed buses, from the noise and hurry of the city. Howth Head was Maggie's favourite walk, so in spite of the weather we drove out there. It was squally out on the Head. The wind took Maggie's scarf and sent it to fly out over the water so fast that we couldn't catch it. The tide was high and waves hit the rocks with a sharp smack. Nobody else was on the headland as we set out for the lighthouse.

"Isn't it grand?" Maggie said as we watched waves climb high on the rocks and fall back to form another attack. Although I had known for months, it was only then I told Maggie that Adele said Daniel could be the father of her child. Too proud to admit I meant so little to Daniel, and because the pain of his betrayal was sharp and fierce still, I hadn't been able to tell her before. She was furious.

"Dirty old bastard," she yelled into the wind. "Wish I could get my hands on him. I'd fix him, I would."

"No point now," I said.

Maggie thumped my arm before ranting about what shits men were as she paced up and down near the cliff edge. Her rage and indignation on my behalf tempered my own anger and humiliation. As it softened a terrible disillusionment crept in. I thought I'd got the worst from Daniel when he deserted me, yet this really stung.

"Well, she doesn't know for sure if it's Daniel's," I said.

Maggie wheeled around and almost lost her footing.

"Come away from there. It's dangerous."

She moved back beside me and we continued out along the headland.

"Whether it is or not isn't the point. The point is it could be."

There was nothing to say to that. A wave crashed against the wall below and a gull rode a wind gust so close to our heads we could see its individual feathers ruffle.

"I'd never have believed it of him. Never. At least not before he left me to face things on my own, anyway. Now I'd believe anything except that he has a heart."

"Well, knowing this changes nothing really, does it? You will still let me have the baby, won't you?"

The discovery of this totally new betrayal of Daniel's made no difference to that, I assured her, she could rest easy.

A man with a Jack Russell on a leash came out from the parking lot and crossed to the edge overlooking the lighthouse. The dog barked once in our direction, then they both turned and walked off away from us.

The wind picked up and a small flock of gulls wheeled and screamed in from the sea. We headed away towards the steeper cliffs, picking up the pace to keep warm. We went a good way out before turning back. In the distance we saw a person coming our way. She walked briskly, head down against the wind, the full skirt of her coat scurrying her along. She was almost on top of us before she looked up. A strand of bright red hair had escaped her headscarf and whipped back and forth in the wind. I recognized Fran Wolfe. Her steps faltered as she recognized us.

"Damn. I should have known we'd run into someone from Kiltilly," I muttered to Maggie, instinctively covering the bulge of my belly.

"You're so wrapped up in that big coat she won't notice. Don't worry."

There was nothing for it but to come face to face. It was the first time I'd seen her since her mother's death, so decency required that I sympathized. Coolly she looked straight at the front of my coat where my bump was.

"Looks like you didn't have much care for my mother," she said. "Sneaking around with my father behind her back. What kind of a woman are you?"

The guilt I felt that my row with Ellen had contributed to her accident rose with a rush, so I said nothing. Maggie spoke up.

"Now wait a minute here. Don't go putting all the blame on my sister. She didn't do it all by herself."

I tried to hush her. She shrugged me off.

"I'm genuinely sorry for your loss. I am," I said.

"You can save your breath. I heard you on the phone with Daniel after she died. Trying to get him to keep on with you in the face of her death."

She tried to push past us.

"One minute there." Maggie reached out to stop her. "You can't talk to my sister like that. And furthermore, that's your half-brother or -sister she's carrying."

"Really? Well, I'd rather have my mother."

She elbowed Maggie in the arm to get past.

"Don't shove me." Maggie stood her ground.

"Get out of my way."

She shouldered into Maggie, who reached out and gave her a push. Fran lost her footing on the wet ground. She threw her arms out to keep herself upright. Maggie made a grab to steady her. She caught Fran's scarf, which came away in her hand. Fran tried to right herself but her feet slithered again on the muddy grass, eyes huge with terror and pleading. Her mouth gaped in horror and with just one single cry she disappeared over the lip of the cliff. Her green and red scarf blew across Maggie's eyes, so at first she didn't see that Fran was gone. I stood frozen for a second or two, then moved gingerly toward the cliff edge. Maggie freed herself from the scarf.

"Where is she?" she asked. "Where did she go?"

I pointed to the cliff.

"She went over."

"Oh my God, is she all right?"

Maggie moved toward the edge.

"Stop. Be careful. It's slippery."

I edged carefully to the lip but couldn't see down to the bottom. The wind whipped my coat around my legs.

"Fran! Fran!" I called.

The wind carried my words back toward to me. I listened before I called again. Only the wind along with the whoosh of breakers answered. I lay down in the soggy earth so I could look over the lip of the cliff. The land fell steeply to sea. Whatever ledges might have broken her fall were covered with water. There was nothing to be seen, only the waves foaming as they dashed themselves on the rock face and surged away from the land. For a second I thought I saw the green plaid of her coat swirling in the water, but that might have been mind over matter. I couldn't be sure.

"Do you see her? Is she there?"

The next gust of wind brought rain with it. Once again I scanned the rock face and then the water. There was no sign at all of Fran. I squirmed back from the edge and got myself to my hands and knees. Maggie came and helped me up to my feet.

"We need to get help. Where will we get help?" Maggie made towards the edge. I caught her arm and stopped her.

"She's not there. She's gone. Just gone. No point putting ourselves in danger too." I held her to me, smearing mud from my coat and hands all over her.

"Jesus, what will we do?"

Maggie's voice was muffled by my shoulder. There was no help to be had. Nobody was around. We could have been the only two people on the planet. Maggie began to tremble against me.

"Let's go back to the village. We can report it there."

"Will they look for her? Jesus! I never meant to kill her." Maggie began to cry. "Oh God, her eyes. I'll never forget them."

"You didn't kill her. It was an accident. We'll report it, but nobody can do much in this storm. The coast guard won't put out tonight, with this weather. Come on, let's go."

I urged her along the path. My legs shook and rain added itself to the wind in earnest. Maggie tried to break out of my hold and go back to the edge again, but I held her fast.

"It's too late. Too late. Come on, let's get out of the cold."

Half dragging my sister, I stumbled my way to the car. I eased her into the passenger seat and dumped my own coat, heavy with mud, into the back seat. I got the engine going and turned the heat up full.

"We have to do something," Maggie said.

Her teeth chattered the words out of her mouth. Fog spread across the windows as the heat kicked in. My hands wouldn't quite obey me when I tried to turn on the wipers.

"We will," I told Maggie. "First we will get warm."

"No, no, we have to get help now. We have to find her."

She grabbed the door handle and fumbled to get out. Before she could, I got the car into gear and eased out of the parking spot. I had intended to stop in the village and report the accident, but I could see Maggie going into shock. I wasn't doing so well myself. The drive back took forever as I tried to keep the car and my mind on the road, Maggie's moans and sobs a terrible backdrop to the horror and confusion that ran inside me. Back at her apartment, I got her into a hot bath and changed into warm dry things myself. What seemed like hours later, but was probably no more than one, Maggie was still in the bath.

"Maggie? You all right in there?"

I knocked on the bathroom door. No answer. I eased the door open. Maggie was still in the bath, knees up to her chin, staring straight ahead.

"You should get out. The water's cold."

She didn't seem to hear me. I grabbed a towel and crouched by the bath.

"Come on, Maggie. Let's get you dressed."

She didn't move until I got her under the arms and eased her up. Once on her feet, she stepped out of the bath when I told her to. I towelled her off and persuaded her into nightclothes. As I tucked her into bed, she finally looked at me.

"Oh God. I killed her, Delia. I killed her."

Tears ran down the edge of her nose. I wiped them with my sleeve.

"It was an accident. It was. I saw it."

Reassurances didn't seem to get through to her. I got her into bed and sat with her till she fell into a restless sleep.

I fully intended to report the accident. The nearest phone box was a few blocks away and it didn't seem a good idea to leave Maggie just then. Besides, it was late night by this time. And I worried about leaving her alone. Next morning she was ill. All day she raved and muttered in a fever as I tried to spoon broth into her. I put off my return to Cardiff and stayed to nurse her until her fever broke and she was well enough to take care of herself. I never did report the accident. Maggie was so ill I couldn't leave her and by the time I could it seemed way too late. Every day I scanned the papers for news of a body being found. There was none. Eventually I went back to Cardiff. The next time I came back to visit, Maggie was reluctant to leave the house. Her terrible slide out of reality had begun.

JUDE AND I BOTH LOST OUR SISTERS THAT DAY. NO MATTER THAT I knew where, precisely, mine was in body, the sister I knew disappeared along with Fran. I whipped up my bitterness against Daniel to bury my own part in destroying both his family and my sister. This was the thing I couldn't say to Jude. I couldn't say it to anyone. It was what went through my mind as Jude wept at the kitchen table and we polished off the whiskey between us.

36

I WOKE WITH A START SOMETIME IN THE EARLY HOURS of the morning. The house was quiet, just a creak of floors settling now and again. I got up to check on Daniel, which had become a habit since he took to his bed permanently. Often I'd find him sleeping, but this night he was awake.

"Do you want company?" I asked.

"Yes, it would be nice."

It was hard to tell whether he was more at peace since the paternity results or if the illness had sapped his energy. He had moved these past days into the state of quiet surrender where energy is used for only essentials. I opened the curtains and the moonlight brightened the unlit room as we sat together.

"Open the window," he asked. "Let the night air in."

I tucked the blankets around him securely to keep out any draughts and threw both sides of the window open as far as they would go. We heard an owl hoot from the trees in the grounds. The occasional engine hum of a car as it passed on the road carried into the room. A breeze came up near dawn and the tree just outside rustled and whispered until the birds began to chirp and trill, covering the sound. Through these hours I held Daniel's hand. We said little. I wanted to tell him again I was sorry, but I knew he would have hushed me. I thought too about our son. Would he have resembled Daniel? He would be a man now, but I saw him that night as the tiny waxen thing I held wrapped in a blue blanket before his body was taken away. Sometime as dawn broke Daniel drifted into sleep. I closed the window and left. I went to my bed and slept until nearly noon.

The following day Jude and I agreed to get a nurse to stay with him at night. He didn't protest. As there was no need of me there all night I once again walked out to the farm in the evenings. Maybe it was because most of my secrets were no longer secret, or maybe it was spending evenings at home with Mam and Da, or maybe it was getting away from the closed world that the Big House had become, but for whatever reason, I noticed a lift in my spirits within days. Once again the beauty of the countryside overtook me as I walked and once again I delighted in the sight of the little farmhouse at the end of my day. Often Iris walked out with me and, as she had with Daniel, she became a favourite of Da's. He even taught her how to milk the cows, an occupation he had guarded fiercely since he had let the big herd go.

After one such visit Iris and I walked back to Daniel's. The first signs of winter were in the air, a chill that nipped at our ears and noses, a faint sheen of frost on the grass.

"Why do you think my mother said Daniel could be my father?" Iris asked.

"She wanted to protect you, just in case Jimmy found her, I think. If she could cast doubt that he was the father she thought you'd be safer. She wanted to keep you safe so much."

She linked her arm in mine and lifted her face to whatever warmth there was in the sun.

"I told Grandma I'll go back to Scotland soon," she said. "I'll wait until Daniel goes. I promised Jude, but I'm ready to be home. I can't stay working in the café the rest of my life. I want to get back to college, settle into our little cottage. My cottage now. I want to find out how to change my name to Iris Sweeney too."

"I'll miss you."

"Oh, Delia, it seems like forever, doesn't it, since I first came? So much has happened. I can hardly believe I have a grandmother and aunties now. And new friends in you and Jude. Do you think you two will be all right? I mean, you'll get back to being friends?"

I watched the crows trail across the sky to their roost. The night I'd found Jude crying over the photograph of Fran, I knew we couldn't possibly be friends, even if she were willing.

"Who knows?" was all I said.

&

"I THINK IT WON'T BE LONG," ANNIE, THE RELIEF NURSE SAID AS she handed over her report. "He's going. I didn't expect it just yet. The doctor was here and upped his morphine. He's calm and not communicative."

"Have you told Jude?"

"She's away out. I didn't know how to get in touch with her. I called you at your place and they told me you were on your way."

I called Mike's number but got no answer. Iris went to look for him on the estate to see if he had any idea where Jude might be. She arrived back with Jude in tow. The two of them sat together with Daniel. After an hour I went to check on him, then went to the kitchen to put on the kettle. Jude followed me.

"How long will it be?"

She seemed calm, but her hands fumbled the tea caddy and tea leaves scattered across the countertop.

"There's no way to tell exactly. The body has its own time. Could be tonight, tomorrow. I think it will be soon."

She nodded and took the tray to his room. I trailed in after her. Daniel was almost as I had left him. His breath was slowing but still regular. I measured out morphine into the syringe and administered it. That done, I took up my place in the parlour again.

Iris came in about twenty minutes later.

"I think he's gone," she said.

&

THE DAY OF THE REMOVAL OF THE REMAINS TO THE CHURCH I went to the funeral home to see Daniel laid out. It was ahead of the appointed hour for the Visitation, so I could have a little time alone with him. He lay in the coffin, hands crossed on his chest. He looked at once recognizable and nothing at all like himself. I pulled up a chair and sat by his body. Here beside him, the time for "if only" was over. There had been no time for our relationship to season and who knew whether or not it would have? As Jude did with ,Fran, I had to let it all go. At least as far as I could. As I sat beside his body, the resentment and anger I'd held against him for so long seemed a waste of time. He was a man trying to do his best, much like the rest of us. To release the power he had in my imagination was a relief. Finally I rose and touched his forehead, patted a stray lock of his hair into place. His skin was cold and hard. Unyielding. From my coat pocket I took the red and green scarf that Maggie had grasped when she tried to steady Fran that day on Howth Head. I ran it through my hands one more time, put it to my nose. The faint trace of her perfume was gone: it smelt slightly musty and of turf smoke from our house. Not much trace of Fran remained. After all this time I had forgiven Daniel, perhaps one day I could forgive myself. I tucked the scarf into the inside breast pocket of Daniel's jacket. For all of us, Fran, Maggie, Jude, and for myself, it was the best I could do. It was all I could do. I had barely smoothed his jacket in place when people began to arrive for the Visitation and the ritual of burial began.

ACKNOWLEDGEMENTS

Many thanks to the following people for their help and support:

Wayde Compton, a true champion of writers, and a patient, thoughtful mentor;

Clarissa Green and Leslie Hill, who read very early drafts and gave me excellent advice and encouragement;

Gayle Mavor, Heather McCabe, Bruce Leighton, Brian O'Neil, and the late Cullene Bryant, part of The Writer's Studio graduate group that read hot-off-my-computer drafts and encouraged me in the final stages of writing this book;

Zsuzsi Gartner, who read the opening pages and gave me excellent advice;

and not least my sister, Una Cotter, without whose input I would have made some very big gaffes;

and to all the folks at Signature Editions for getting this story out into the world in such a beautiful form.

ABOUT THE AUTHOR

JOAN B. FLOOD GREW UP IN LIMERICK, IRELAND AND LIVED briefly in France and England before settling in Canada. She spent a number of years in Ottawa, Toronto and Hamilton, before putting down roots in Vancouver, where she currently lives. She has published a Young Adult novel *New Girl.* Her poetry, short fiction, and non-fiction have been published in the literary journals and anthologies *Room of One's Own, By Word of Mouth, Emerge* (Canada), *Lesbian Bedtime Stories,* the *Binnacle Ninth Annual Ultra-Short Story Competition* 2012 edition (USA), and *Wee Girls: Women Writing from an Irish Perspective* (Australia). Her YA novel *New Girl* (Musa Publishing, USA), won the Orpheus Fiction Contest and her story "87" won honourable mention in The Binnacle Ninth Annual Ultra-Short Story Competition. A graduate of Simon Fraser University's The Writer's Studio (TWS), she spends time in nature and visits art galleries and photo exhibits. Otherwise she hangs out in coffee shops, where she people watches and scribbles in notebooks.